DEFINING INTELLIGENCE

In An Educational Context

Dr. Pat Keogh

authorHOUSE®

AuthorHouse™
1663 Liberty Drive
Bloomington, IN 47403
www.authorhouse.com
Phone: 1-800-839-8640

First published by AuthorHouse 06/25/2014

ISBN: 978-1-4567-7634-3 (sc)
ISBN 978-1-4567-9752-2 (hc)
ISBN: 978-1-4969-8555-2 (e)

Printed in the United States of America

Any people depicted in stock imagery provided by Thinkstock are models,
and such images are being used for illustrative purposes only.
Certain stock imagery © Thinkstock.

This book is printed on acid-free paper.

Newgrange; an enduring testament to human Intelligence

Newgrange megalithic burial tomb in County Meath, Ireland is 5200 years old (more than 500 years older than the pyramids of Egypt). It was skilfully constructed. A low, narrow 19 metres long tunnel or passage, with gigantic stone slabs and boulders on either side supporting a roof of equally large slabs, leads to a central chamber. Three burial cells extend out from the chamber to the north, west and south; cruciform in design. This inner sanctuary is enclosed by a corbelled stone structure, 6 metres high, with a large capstone on top and two metres of stones over that. Water channels are chiselled at various points in the corbelling ensuring that the chamber and cells are totally water proof. How our early ancestors masterfully engineered and achieved their objectives, and, managed to lift and set in place those enormous slabs and boulders is unfathomable.

A large flat slab closes the entrance. In front of that lies a magnificently decorated entrance boulder. The triple spiral is the predominant feature of this stone, probably representing a cyclical order of birth, life and a spiritual afterlife. Along the bottom of the boulder is a rippling carving believed to represent the nearby river Boyne, their main source of water and principle means of travel. This remarkable, enduring art work required patient, laborious chiselling, hacking and scraping.

Directly above the entrance is an aperture that allows light from the early morning rising sun at mid-winter to enter the tomb. This is the most awesome feature of the edifice. The sheer ingenuity and skill in precision alignment of the aperture, passage and inner chamber with winter solstice sunrise is amazing. Sun-rays spear through the aperture then stealthily creep up the long, narrow passage and illuminate the inner chamber for 17 minutes. The concept is ingenious. It must have taken decades of planning, observing and mapping the path of the sun rays even before the back-breaking, laborious execution of the intellectual concept began. Executing the concept posed a serious challenge since clouds frequently cover the rising sun during the mid-winter period in Ireland. Furthermore, our Neolithic ancestors had a short life span. They rarely lived beyond thirty three years. Despite those obstacles, the engineering and architectural execution of the concept is awesome.

We can only surmise the thoughts that inspired this monumental creation. They probably believed that the souls of those whose ashes lay in stone bowels in the inner cells would be enlivened by the sun's illumination at Winter Solstice. You can be mystified here; experiencing a presence that is absent or an absence that is present. You become cosmologically aware and experience a still, silent, existential moment in an eternal, effusive, cyclical order.

Newgrange Neolithic people may have viewed this tomb, which they covered over with clay and grass sods to form a mound, as a symbol of pregnant earth. The sun spears life through the passage into the womb of the dark, dormant tomb, awakening and impregnating it, and, simultaneously enlightening slumbering souls. The Autumnal Equinox, nine months later, heralds the end of gestation. The earth gives birth following the pains of harvest-time labour. She produces bountiful resources to sustain life. Then she rests. The sun at the next Winter Solstice will illuminate, impregnate and set life in motion once more. The spiritual and material worlds coexist in perpetual, blissful harmony.

I dedicate this book to the memory of my mother,
Margaret Keogh

&

To Nora and our family for their support and
patience while I researched material for this work

CONTENTS

Acknowledgements. xiii

Preface xv

Introduction xvii

Chapter 1 - Who Am I?
The mind and the brain in an historical context *1*

Chapter 2 - Cogito, Ergo Sum, & Science
Language and thinking 23

Chapter 3 - *Historicity & Personality*
The unconscious mind *41*

Chapter 4 - Thinking
Conditioning, indoctrination and education. *61*

Chapter 5 - Defining Intelligence
Emotional Intelligence & Multiple Intelligence *81*

Chapter 6 - Education, Wisdom & IQ
Teach the body, heed the mind. *103*

Glossary **123**

Bibliography. **133**

Index **139**

ACKNOWLEDGEMENTS

Gabhaim buíochas don Ollamh Oideachais, Séan P.Ó Mathúna, a thug treoir dom nuair a bhí mé ag déanamh taighde ar 'smaointeoireacht criticiúil', i gColáiste na hOllscoile, B.Á.C.

I express my gratitude to Francis Hugo and Portia Peterson of AuthorHouse publishers, for the assistance they gave me during the final stages of designing and publishing this work.

To Joan Pickering I offer sincere thanks. Joan typed the original manuscript, and many modifications subsequently, often working late at night in so doing.

Thanks too, to Jennifer Slaybaugh of Authorhouse for her assistance with designing the front cover of the book.

Those who study philosophy are intrigued by the complexity of the human mind and the elements that constitute intelligence. Three factors, (I) *Intelligence Quotient* assessments (II) Theories of *Emotional Intelligence* and *Multiple Intelligences,* and, (III) Research on *Critical Thinking,* have prompted me to inquire into the concept *mind* and to seek a definition of intelligence.

As Principal teacher of a large Dublin suburban primary school for the past twenty three years I have read numerous psychological assessment reports purporting to present children's level of intelligence. Those tests are devised in accordance with the perceived view of how the majority of people reason and behave. From the results of those assessments the participant is awarded a quotient, a number denoting the measure of his/ her intelligence. We may need to question the validity of any test devised to measure human intelligence.

The theories of *Multiple Intelligences* and *Emotional Intelligence* may require analysis too. Those theories appear to give the impression that the meaning of human intelligence has been discovered. We need to establish what those theories tell us about intelligence and the thinking process.

Studies on what *Critical thinking entails* and a realization of the categorical distinction between the process and the product of thinking have highlighted the necessity for an analytical evaluation of human thinking. Scientific research and philosophical investigation are also required in order to clarify the meaning of intelligence.

The word *Intelligence* is used in such broad and varied contexts that its meaning is vague and ambiguous. Contrary positions are adopted by contemporary educational philosophers in their pursuance of a definition of intelligence. There are *those* who aim to establish precise limits to intelligence. They set out to categorise every individual, to place each person at a point on a scale. Others subscribe to a totally open-ended definition of intelligence. For them almost any talent a person possesses is deemed to be an intelligence of some sort.

In searching for a definition and an understanding of human intelligence we may be drawn into deeper and more fundamental questions that belong to the discipline of metaphysics. What is the mind? Is the mind distinct from the body? Can we establish the origin and destination of the mind? Can the mind exist apart from the body? Two opposing philosophical perspectives produce very different answers to those questions. On the one hand we have theorists who recognise a material reality only, on the other are those who maintain that a spiritual reality directs and controls the material world.

Those who believe only in a material reality maintain that nature controls everything. We are part of nature. The mind is an essential dimension of the human person. Thinking is as natural to humans as swimming is to fish or flying to birds. We are part of the evolutionary process. Earthquakes, storms, rain, sunshine, growth and decay are natural phenomena. Minute microscopic organisms, bacteria and viruses, big and powerful creatures, the lion, the shark and the whale as well as birds, insects and of course human beings all play their part in the evolutionary process. The human contribution to evolution may be no better than that of the earthworm. The earthworm eats earth and decaying vegetation and then excretes it. In doing this it aerates and fertilizes the soil so that crops grow better. Consequently, other creatures, including humans secure food.

Humans have inflicted, and continue to inflict a great deal of destruction on the earth by poisoning the soil, the vegetation, the water and the atmosphere with chemicals, pesticides, insecticides and pollution from industrial waste. Other creatures do not inflict such damage.

We have a mind, but, for those who accept a material reality only, the mind is nothing more than animal instinct. It obeys the laws of nature like everything else. If I invent something great that benefits humankind or improves the earth that invention will help to maintain the balance of nature. The invention is as transitory as the inventor. I did not choose my arrival on the earth. I am a slave of nature and I do her bidding. I have no extraordinary powers. They may appear extraordinary to me but in the context of universal order they are insignificant. I appear infinitely great by comparison with microscopic beings but am infinitely small when compared to the vastness of the universe.

From the *Spiritual* perspective there exists an outside force that controls the universe and all things in it. The material world and natural evolution are directed and maintained in harmony through a supreme intelligence. Human intelligence endeavours to control the material world in so far as it affects our development as humans. There may be other intelligent beings on other planets operating through the influence and guidance of this *Supreme Intelligence*. In general, we can accept that nature controls itself. It seems that evolution requires no outside assistance. Nature's balancing methods appear to check and direct the evolutionary process. However, there may be a spiritual force that influences the course of nature.

The human being has both a material and a spiritual dimension. In life the person is attracted to and influenced by material, physical and spiritual forces. Our education system ought to cater for the welfare and development of all the dimensions of the person. The creative and imaginative dimension of the child's life needs to be fostered. In order to do this, the teacher ought to enable each student to express him/herself in music, art, drama and dance. The child should be given time to invent, compose and create and also time to think, analyse, reflect and daydream. Metaphysics must not be the preserve of an elite minority.

The material aspect of the person should be catered for in our education system. Self awareness and awareness of the environment are crucial aspects of teaching and learning. Good communication techniques ought to be developed. Economics and science are important but they should not be awarded unbridled prominence in the curriculum. In contemporary pedagogy; trade, commerce and science appear to be afforded pride of place.

In our education systems we do not have to divorce the mental dimension of the person from the material. However, from a philosophical perspective and in an attempt to define and understand human intelligence, we may need to examine the mental and material aspects of the person separately. The role of education is not solely to cater for our material needs.

Religion and spiritual education are viewed by some as divisive and irrelevant in modern living. Others hold the contrary view believing that spiritual and religious education ought to permeate the whole curriculum. Teachers may try to avoid taking a stance on one side or the other. However, what teachers teach and how they teach may very well determine their beliefs.

Have we a right to condition or indoctrinate children? Conditioning is unacceptable if it is used to mould an individual for some sinister purpose i.e. to get him/her to fit neatly into an ordered consumer, materialist society. Yet conditioning may be necessary in order to train very young children in matters relating to health, safety and hygiene, where rational methods may not be possible.

Indoctrination is wrong. It involves one person using his/her will to control or force another to accept a belief without allowing the other to use his/her reason to consider acceptance or rejection of the belief.

Education involves establishing truth and objectivity through logical and rational arguments. It should aim to establish situations where students can create and discover and have time and opportunities to analyse and judge events and statements. Teaching children to be analytical must be a primary objective of every education system. The role of the educator is to enable students to acquire knowledge and ultimately to attain wisdom.

Beliefs do not need to be empirically verifiable. Many beliefs are not dependent on the senses or the material world. It is not unreasonable for a person to inquire into and to engage in metaphysical issues and to believe in a spiritual reality.

We ought to be able to define the words and terms we use. We may not fully comprehend the limits of a concept denoted by a word but we should be able to define it, nevertheless. The word *infinity* is one of those concepts. God, eternity and nothingness are others. The word *intelligence* is often used in a very broad and loose sense. We need to clarify some of the misconceptions about the meaning of intelligence.

A contemporary philosopher of education, Howard Gardner, has produced a theory claiming that humans possess multiple intelligences. This theory, however, does not define intelligence. It leaves it open to further definition and interpretation. Gardner's *Multiple Intelligence* theory appears to equate intelligence with skill.

We may need to question *Intelligence Quotient Tests* and other attempts to measure intelligence too. It may be unethical to set limits to, or set tests to measure another human being's intelligence. *Intelligence Tests* may measure knowledge, experience attained through the senses and the capability of the senses to acquire knowledge as well as the behaviour patterns of a person. We may be able to measure some of the results of intelligence, but, can we measure intelligence per se?

Language is a vital dimension of psychological assessments. Verbal language is a human characteristic essentially, and, it is human intelligence that we have under the microscope here, metaphorically speaking. If human language is equated with thinking and if we can assess the language level achieved by an individual then we may be able to assess the thinking ability of that person. The problem is to assess the process of thinking. Measuring the level of a person's acquired verbal language or his/her ability to use verbal language in set tests may tell us how much that person has learned or how much lived experience s/he has acquired. This will give an indication of the person's ability to learn and to use his/her thinking power to achieve results. But such assessments do not measure intelligence. Non verbal tests have more validity but too many other factors influence the result.

St. Augustine at the beginning of the fifth century awarded priority to the human mind over the body with the words, 'Even if I am mistaken, I am'. In the seventeenth century Rene Descartes' *'Cogito, ergo sum, ergo, sum res cogitans'* (I think, therefore I am, therefore I am a thinking being) further emphasised this idea. He set out to establish thinking as the essential dimension of the person. Gilbert Ryle, a twentieth century British philosopher, in **The Concept of Mind** tried to disestablish Descartes' thesis. Ryle proclaimed the idea of the mind as separate from the body to be a myth. He rejected the notion of a mind/body dualism.

We need to clarify the distinction between *knowledge, intelligence* and *wisdom*. We acquire knowledge and wisdom. We do not acquire intelligence. Intelligence helps us to acquire knowledge and to convert knowledge to wisdom. Wisdom is gained through experience and acquired knowledge. Intelligence involves thinking and thinking is conducted through language.

The most notable philosopher of language of the twentieth century, Ludwig Wittgenstein, in his two most famous works ***Tractatus Logico-Philosophicus*** and ***Philosophical Investigations,*** sees language and thinking as identical. We cannot think without language and we cannot use language without thinking. Wittgenstein denounces the notion of the existence of *a private language* or *inner thinking* divorced from language in everyday use. His whole philosophy revolved around the inseparability of thought and language. Gilbert Ryle, a contemporary of Wittgenstein's, centred his philosophy on the inseparability of mind and body. Wittgenstein was concerned with the thinking person.

Perhaps we cannot measure intelligence but we may be able to define it. Our starting point ought to be an investigation into the relationship between the human mind and the brain. *Who am I?* Is a question that cannot be answered by an objective assessor. However, I, the subject, may hold the key to an answer to that question. In our quest for a comprehensive understanding of intelligence we must examine human thinking.

We distinguish between pure, *a priori* thinking and responsive, *a posteriori thinking.* A priori thinking is creative thinking. It is the ability to compose, create, invent and, it involves the ability to contemplate abstract ideas and metaphysical issues. It also includes the ability to disengage from the material world. This disengagement affords the unconscious mind freedom to meditate, to drift and to take control of the material world.

A posteriori thinking is at a lower level. It responds to information received through the senses. This thinking is dependent on the physical, material world with goals and a modus operandi that revolve around the continuance of the species, the survival of the human race. *A posteriori* thinking is not far removed from instinct in animal life. It has evolved and continues to evolve as a result of knowledge and experience acquired from living in the world.

CHAPTER 1

WHO AM I?
The mind and the brain in an historical context

We cannot verify the existence of the human mind through empirical methods, from an examination of human evolution or brain activity nor can we define human intelligence by observing a person's behaviour, character or personality.

The brain is the mainspring of the human body. Centres exist in the brain that account for the articulation, decoding and comprehension of speech and language. The brain receives messages through the senses and it reacts to sense experiences. Rapidly expanding information on the capability of the brain has led many to believe that the brain thinks and that the brain is the mind. Edward de Bono says: "For the first time in human history we can relate thinking directly to the behaviour of the brain."[1]

A person is often defined in terms of brainpower, the brain is the person, or, the person is the brain. A well developed, nourished, regularly stimulated, healthy brain seems to have greater thinking ability than the brain that receives insufficient exercise, stimulation and nourishment in the same way as the fit, supple, well nourished body performs with greater agility and power than the unfit body. The brain needs oxygen, water and food in order to function and even to survive just like any other part of the body. It is a material body part. Its dimensions are measurable and observable. It has a colour, shape, size and weight.

There are some things about the person, however, that we cannot observe or measure. We cannot measure mood, sorrow, joy, happiness or depression. There are other aspects of the person too, that we cannot measure, such as commitment to a cause, use of the imagination and one's levels of faith, hope and love.

In *The Concept of Mind* [2] Gilbert Ryle claimed that there is nothing mysterious, elusive or magical about the mind. The person is simply the person in all his/her doings and dimensions, thinking, acting, communicating, reasoning, willing, judging etc. We do not need to waste valuable time in trying to look beyond what we see. From an assessment of what people do or have done we can conclude that all humans act similarly in similar situations.

The person, according to Ryle, is not a body with a soul. There is no Ghost in the machine. The person is what we see, nothing more or less. The fact that we are different to all other creatures on earth is a fact of nature. Fish are not birds. They are a different species. This fact takes the mystery away from the idea that the human being belongs to a unique and privileged species. Being of a unique species is also the privilege of hedgehogs. The vast majority of contemporary scientists and many philosophers too, have come to the conclusion that we are a product of evolution just like all other creatures on earth.

In the *Origin of Species* [3] written in the middle of the nineteenth century, Charles Darwin questioned accepted beliefs concerning the creation of the world and the creation of the human race. Darwin's theory of evolution had profound effects on people's thinking and led to a change in their religious beliefs and convictions during his lifetime and ever since. This change subsequently led to a revision of philosophical, religious and scientific teaching and research. Before Darwin's time people believed that God created the world about six thousand years ago. Darwin maintained that the earth is three million years in existence. Today, Geologists maintain that the earth is more than four and a half billion years old.

Before formulating his theory of evolution Charles Darwin spent some time observing bird life on the Galapagos archipelago, volcanic islands off the coast of Ecuador. Giant tortoises live on many of the islands. Those tortoises have significant differences on the various islands. The differences result mainly from the food supply available on a particular island and the manner in which the tortoises obtain their food. On one of the islands the tortoises have to stretch their necks to reach food high up on rocks. To enable them to do that their shell has taken on a saddle shape which allows greater mobility of the neck. Tortoises on other islands do not need to go to such lengths to obtain food

Change occurs on the Galapagos archipelago more rapidly and much more noticeably than on any other part of the earth. Those islands are moving in a South Easterly direction at a rate of five to seven centimetres per year. They have moved about ten metres since Darwin's time. The birth and decay of the islands as well as the manner in which birds, land animals and marine life exist and evolve, mainly through adaptation to environmental conditions and the survival of the fittest, gave Darwin the idea and the basis upon which to establish his theory of evolution. As Darwin travelled from island to island he observed that finches had some obvious noticeable differences on each of the islands. One particular observable difference was the shape of their beaks. The beak variations resulted from the manner in which the finch acquired food. This led him to conclude that they all came originally from the same species of finch. Variations occurred as they adapted to different conditions in order to obtain food. Eventually, some were classified as new species. At least thirteen different species of finch exist on the Galapagos archipelago today.

Darwin also looked at animal embryos and discovered that human and many animal embryos look alike at the early gestation stage in their mother's womb. From this observation he concluded that we are distant relatives of those animals. Earlier research in zoology had discovered that the different species of animals had developed characteristics specific to their needs. In Darwin's time many scientists had come to accept that skills and characteristics acquired by individuals, through their own efforts and discoveries, were passed on to the succeeding generation. Darwinian theories illuminated by subsequent evolutionary discoveries and research, prompted philosophers and scientists to delve deeper into seeking the origin of the universe, and, the origin of the human mind.

Is it a supreme intelligence, or, a big bang that is responsible for the creation of the world? We may need to look at this question from evolutionary, historical, scientific and philosophical perspectives. The

Big Bang theory, accepted today by many scientists, postulates that all creation started with a big bang that occurred thirteen point seven billion years ago. At that time an immeasurable mass of indeterminate matter existed. Through gravity and a build up of intense heat this mass of matter exploded causing an enormous bang that sent huge chunks of matter flying out in all directions.

A project by European scientists, conducted recently in a tunnel beneath the Alps in Switzerland to simulate the big bang still awaits detailed analysis of the material following their controlled explosion. The big bang explosion allegedly set in motion our constellation of stars and the millions of other constellations that exist in the universe today. New stars and planets on other solar systems within our constellation are being discovered frequently with the aid of telescopes that are constantly being improved in magnification and focus clarity. The next phase in the development of infrared telescopes may open up a whole new world of stars and planets to us. This will compel us to probe even deeper into the unfathomable mystery of the universe.

Recent astronomical discoveries of planets Gliese 581c and Gliese 581d, in the Libra constellation, first discovered April 2007 [4] are thought by scientists to be capable of sustaining life. Scientists are getting closer to finding another earth-like planet. Planet Gliese 581d is 20 light years away from earth and its mass is nearly twenty times that of our planet. In late April 2009 the team of scientists observing this planet claimed that it is within the habitable zone where water and consequently life could exist.

Some of the stars and their satellite planets are millions of light years away. If a person was on one of those planets today, for instance, looking towards our planet that person would be looking at the earth as it existed millions of years back in time, long before humans lived on earth. This leaves us as eager to speculate on the past as to predict the future.

Recording time is a human invention. If existence and existents are in a cyclical time frame the past may be as relevant as the future. If living beings and objects exist in a linear time order, as the *Big Bang* theory suggests, the past has little relevance, the future is all important, evolution will continue for all eternity. From the perspective of the mind the past is as important as the future. We constantly seek guidance from the past to make decisions about the future. In our daily living we rely on our memory as much as on our insight. Our reliance on the past prepares us for the future.

According to those who accept the big bang theory, the matter that was propelled outwards at an enormous speed following the explosion are now planets, solar systems and constellations and they will continue to fly outwards as they have ever since that big bang of over thirteen billion years ago. This movement away from that centre will continue for all eternity.

Logically, the *Big Bang* theory must conclude that all substances; solids, liquids, gases and all mammals, reptiles, fish, birds, bacteria as well as the material substance of every star and planet evolved from the original matter that existed before the explosion. The Ancient Greek philosophers Thales and Anaximander believed that everything that exists has a basic underlying common substance. Parmenides (540 - 480 BC) held the view that everything that now exists always existed. He held that change is impossible, reality is undivided and homogenous.

In pre-philosophical and pre-scientific times myths and magic guided and dominated a great deal of human thinking. Many people today believe that the notion of an all powerful God is a myth. Where did this God come from? Others believe that the Big Bang theory too, is a myth. A lot of gaps would need to be filled in order to make credible the evolutionary process that commenced with a big bang explosion and eventually produced an intelligent human race. Furthermore, the cause, and composition of the matter that exploded would need explanation. The cause of the extreme heat that ignited and forced all the matter to move outward forming the universe with its stars and planets and subsequently set the universe in perfect harmony requires explanation too. This theory could be viewed as a contemporary perspective on the notion of a single substance from which everything is made; a similar view to that of the ancient Greek philosophers Thales and Anaximander.

Plato, (427 - 347 BC) who has probably had the greatest influence over western philosophy postulated that ***prime matter*** is the basic stuff from which everything is made; all substantial forms have a basic underlying prime matter. This prime matter could be compared to modelling clay from which we can make any form; a cat, person, house, tree, etc. De Spinoza, a Dutch philosopher of the seventeenth century produced a similar idea. He maintained that there is only one basic substance in the world. He called this, simply, ***substance.***

Philosophy, as a subject domain or area of inquiry, is afforded less research time and commands much less interest in contemporary times than in the past. This is a mistake, for, while many philosophical and theoretical myths have been dispelled through scientific discoveries many philosophical questions still remain unanswered. Besides, it is through philosophical reasoning that new problems, ideas, issues and questions are raised that require investigation, analysis and answers. The answers may need to be verified or falsified. The first step in the solution to any problem is to recognise it as a problem. This is followed by a clear expression or articulation of the problem. If we do not recognise a problem then we cannot express it or state what it is. If we cannot state clearly what the problem is then it is very difficult to solve it.

Philosophy must continue to seek answers to unresolved metaphysical questions relating to the origin of the universe and the origin of life, and, whether there exists a spiritual, mental world distinct and separate from a material, physical world. Another important philosophical question relates to *my role* in the world. Am 'I' in control and master of the material world around me, or, am 'I' a product of my surrounding physical, material world? A definitive answer to those questions would be the key to unlocking the mystery pertaining to the definition of intelligence. The person is more than the combination of all the functions of the body and the brain. The whole is greater than the sum of its parts.

Do I shape and adapt the material world to my needs or does the material world mould and shape me? The vast majority of contemporary scientists and philosophers maintain that the world moulds me. It was there before my coming into it and it will be there after I have departed. I am born into a particular part of the earth with its climate, atmosphere, culture, language and heritage. Natives of the Congo are likely to be black in skin colour. Natives of Iceland are likely to have white skin. We are born with particular features and of a particular gender.

We may be able to change or arrange to have changed during life many of the features that we are born with. But there are some things like our DNA type that we have no control over. The environment into which we are born determines one's role in life to a great extent too. The type of work we engage in, the social, political and religious lifestyle we become involved in are all influenced by our environment and by external circumstances.

We depend on the earth's resources for water, air and food. All of this pertains to the material world.

Have we any insight into the world of the mind? If human intelligence is something other than brain activity then is that intelligence linked to a supreme being? This is a fundamental philosophical question. Human intelligence gives us a uniqueness and superiority over other creatures on earth. Humans are trying to control human life, deciding its origin and destiny. Birth control, abortion, euthanasia, cloning and the most recent alleged creation of artificial life, synthetic DNA (many genetic scientists dispute the notion that life of any type was created in those experiments) could be seen as methodical steps aiming to produce a perfect human race. In the late nineteenth century, a German philosopher, Friedrich Nietzsche[5] wrote of the necessity for humanity to strive for perfection, shed servitude to Religion and develop strength of will power. He sought the perfect human race and spoke of the creation of *ubermensch*, the superman.

Adolf Hitler, the German dictator of the twentieth century set about producing the perfect human race disposing of people who were physically weak or mentally challenged and allowing the strongest to dominate. Hitler's regime could be seen as an enactment of the Darwinian principle of the survival of the fittest and simultaneously the creation of the Nietzschean *ubermensch*. Nietzsche's superman, however, was meant to be a superior being more in the intellectual than in the physical sense. Hitler's regime was established and driven by physical force and material power. He was less concerned with the human mind or with the intellectual or artistic qualities of the person. Hitler's attempts to establish a world devoid of invalids, geriatrics and the mentally ill were condemned vehemently after the Second World War. Today, in laboratories and hospitals in some parts of the world, albeit unauthorised, a similar end is being sought, but in a humane manner i.e. different means to attain the same end.

The mind, it appears, is the distinguishing characteristic that separates the human being from all other creatures on earth. Nevertheless, it is universally accepted nowadays that the human being, like other animals, is a product of evolution. The human being has evolved through the ages. We have invented sophisticated communication systems. We have altered many aspects of the earth and our environment to cater for and ensure our survival. We can survive beneath the water, (in submarines) in space (in space ships) and in places with the most extreme weather conditions on earth, from hottest Africa to frozen Antarctica. This type of adaptation is no more than a survival and evolutionary trait. It is meditation on the meaning of life, the search for an understanding of the origin and destination of the human mind and the ability to inquire into an existence beyond the material world that is unparalleled. Human intelligence can analyse the past as well as plan for the future.

The argument for believing that the brain is the all important factor in human existence stems mainly from the *Theory of Evolution*. Three stages in the evolution of the human brain can be clearly identified. The brain-stem is the reptilian brain. Reptiles have a simple brain that controls bodily movements including reflex action, reproductive urges, blood circulation, digestion, respiration and survival of the species. The brain-stem is connected to the nervous system. The second stage in the evolution of the brain was the growth of the cortex on top of the (brain stem) reptilian brain. This is the mammalian brain. It controls the emotions, the hormones, sexual urges, body temperature and other mammalian functions. Finally: the neo-cortex grew on top of the cortex. This is the most recent stage in the evolutionary development of the human brain.

It is in the neo-cortex that thinking, planning, analysing and creating takes place. The neo-cortex controls language, communication, speech, art creation, music composition, appreciation of the arts and other specifically human activities. The development of the neo-cortex has enabled us to control many of our basic feelings and to plan for a future. The emotional brain seeks immediate pleasure and avoidance of suffering. The rational brain can allow us to endure pain and suffering and refuse to indulge in immediate gratification in the hope or belief of future rewards and benefits.

In recent times, since about 5000 B.C. we, humans have learned to influence and exercise some control over evolution and adapt it to our own needs. Prehistoric people could distinguish between the weak, slow, lazy horse and the strong, fast, energetic one. They could also distinguish the good from the bad hunting dog, the cow that produces a lot of milk and the one that gives little milk, the hen that lays lots of eggs and the hen that lays little or no eggs. The productive and stronger types were kept for breeding. This trend of nurturing the creatures that are most beneficial to us continues to this day.

Contemporary scientific experiments in cloning as well as the collection and storing of human female eggs and male sperm from the strongest, brightest and most disease free may be but another step in human evolution. It is another attempt to establish the *ubermensch*. This may be human's way of ensuring the survival of the fittest.

The human brain has evolved at a much greater rate, and it has risen to a far superior level, than has the brain of any other creature on earth. "During every minute of the nine months of pregnancy the brain gains a quarter of a million brain cells. The brain is genetically hard-wired to produce a staggering total of around 100 billion neurons and a trillion glial cells which provide all the necessary support and protection: This will lead to a multi-trillion network capable of performing twenty million billion calculations per second." [6]

The 100 billion neurons with which the child is born does not increase as s/he grows into adulthood. At birth, however, there is little or no contact between many of these neurons but, as the brain develops communication increases. This is brought about through myelinization, a lubrication process that produces cohesion and collaboration between cells. The brain develops very rapidly during the early years of childhood. Full maturation and cell cohesion gives the brain tremendous capability and power. Because of this incomprehensible potential many believe that the brain is the defining aspect of the person.

Let us examine some of the functions of the brain and in particular areas that are associated with thinking. We acknowledge, initially, that the brain is the driving force behind all bodily functions. It is the powerhouse that receives and interprets sensations. It initiates perceptions. It controls and directs reflexes and reactions.

The brain has a left and a right hemisphere. It is contained within the skull casing. The right hemisphere of the brain appears to be more involved with emotional arousal, curbing stress and survival than the left hemisphere. The brain is involved in directing and controlling the five senses. The brain is involved too, in decoding, making sense of, and, utilising data received via the senses.

The left side of the brain controls the right side of the body. The right side of the brain controls the left side of the body. The right is assumed to be the creative side. The left side is taken to be the logical side. Science has shown that the left hemisphere responds to speech sounds from a very early age in the child's development while the right hemisphere responds more to non-human sounds, squeaks, drumming sounds and music. It is the left side that detects speech changes, a person's accent and tone of voice. Reading, writing, speaking and understanding reside in the left side. The right side controls art and music and is involved in deciphering the meanings of sentences. In the right side, too, sentences are placed in context.

A person with damage to the right hemisphere will have reduced levels of attention. The right hemisphere also appears to show more sensitivity to pain then the left. Conversations heard in the right ear are processed in the left hemisphere, which is the language side of the brain. In general, speech sounds entering the right ear can be processed, retained and consequently repeated more accurately than those entering the left ear. Music and other sounds from nature and the environment are more accurately received and processed when presented through the left ear.

The cerebrum is the area of the brain where most conscious operations occur. It is composed of four pairs of lobes; the **frontal, temporal, parietal** and **occipital**, a left and right of each. The frontal lobes direct voluntary bodily movement, both basic and skilled movement. Emotions and behaviour are restrained and controlled here. Speech, taste and smell are received, comprehended and deciphered in the frontal lobes and a response is given to sensations from these lobes. The left frontal lobe is calculating, it creates complicated plans and it is responsible for the execution of those plans. It plays a major role in speech and language comprehension. This lobe of the brain is precise, logical, analytical and controlling. It is unfeeling.

For a child with speech and language difficulties beneficial results should be gained from presenting speech via the right ear which is processed in the left frontal lobe. Initally, the child's level of hearing in both ears must be established. If one ear presents with a hearing loss sounds entering the better hearing ear will be directed to the appropriate area to be processed. There is constant cooperation and collaboration between both sides of the brain.

Teachers, speech and language therapists, and parents might consider getting children to wear headphones with a silent left ear cover and a right ear receiver that conveys appropriate and easily comprehended oral language. It may be even more effective and advantageous, depending on the subject matter and the particular child, to have appropriate and complimentary music channelled into the left ear piece while oral language is voiced through the right ear. This method would be of particular advantage in teaching the lyrics and the melody of a song simultaneously. Using both sides of the brain to the highest potential possible and in the right circumstances will achieve maximum results for the learner. This approach could be highly effective particularly in teaching history, storytelling to young children and in explaining culture differences to pupils. It could be effective too, in teaching mathematics and science, particularly where the factual information entering the right ear can be enlivened and made more attractive by means of appropriate, complementary, stimulating, harmonious and rhythmic sounds entering the left ear.

The right frontal lobe is considered to be more in tune with nature. It views events in a holistic way. It is more involved with sensory perception than with abstract thinking. This is the creative side of the brain. Encouraging more activity in the right frontal lobe gives the analytical left frontal lobe time to rest, time to pause before delivering a response, and, consequently adding a certain flavour (humour, wit etc.) to that response.

Oral language and other sounds entering through the ears are received by the organ of Corti in the inner ear. Vibrations caused by sounds travelling along the cochlear duct are converted into nerve impulses and transmitted through the auditory nerve to the thalamus, temporal and frontal lobes. If unwelcome sounds, perceived to be harmful to us are heard, a message is immediately sent to the limbic system for a reaction. The result may be panic, fright or an emotional outburst. The amygdala situated in the limbic system, prompts us to act or to give an emotional reaction.

Recent research has shown that apart from this route of ears to thalamus to temporal lobes to amygdala, sometimes a direct route from ears to thalamus to amygdala operates to produce a more immediate emotional reaction. By allowing a time lapse the sound message will be sent to the frontal lobes for a calculated and analytical response. The parietal lobes deal with touch sensation in a similar manner. The occipital lobes react to what we see and to what we recognise through sight. The eyes, like the ears, are but receivers.

The senses are the mediators that create the contact between the brain and the outside material world. Sight recognition, colour identification, movement of objects and the processing of visual information take place in the occipital lobes. That recognition is linked with former knowledge and through that linkage it is retained in the memory. In the temporal lobes comprehension of spoken words, attention, identification and categorisation of objects and recognition of people's faces are processed. The parietal lobes are concerned with spatial orientation, hand-eye coordination, tactile awareness and awareness of body parts. The cerebellum controls fine motor coordination, posture, balance and eye movement, involuntary movement including respiration, blood circulation, heart beat and the ability to walk.

Messages or sensations entering through the various senses are processed initially in the lobes specific to the sense and then transferred to the frontal lobes where decisions are made, some instantaneously on the action, reaction or response required. Some decisions on data received through the senses, however, are not given instantaneously. A delay may occur, allowing a more logical and reasoned response. Information deemed important is deliberately stored in the memory-bank for later recall when or if required.

The brain stem assists the cerebellum in the control of involuntary movement. It is connected to the spinal cord. The spinal cord is the main communication line linking the brain and all body parts. Through it, messages are sent to stimulate and control the various systems of the body both voluntary and involuntary functioning, and, to direct conscious bodily movement

The brain controls and directs the whole body including the operation of the various parts of the brain itself. When a person is declared brain-dead, that person is considered dead even though the body can be kept going with the aid of a life support machine. After death the various elements and compounds that make up the material body return to the earth and are recycled as the body decays. The frontal lobes are the thinking, reasoning, planning and analysing organs. Consequently, death of the frontal lobes means death of the person to all effective purposes. Can we deduce from that that the frontal lobes are the seat of intellectual activity and that this is essentially the mind?

It could be argued that the mind directs the brain. The brain then directs the rest of the body. The controversy over which is the centre of the person's intelligence and creativity, the mind or the brain, has been teased out over the centuries but without a definitive conclusion. Scientific research has dispelled many of the myths about the mind. Likewise, metaphysicians and spiritualists have exposed many mysteries that contemporary science is unable to explain.

Does the mind of the person use the senses to make sense of the material world, or, is it the senses that supply the mind with information on the material world, and, the mind then makes use of that information, converts it to knowledge and stores it for later use? For those who take the brain to be the mind that question is irrelevant. The brain is the mind. For those who do not accept this, an understanding of the complexity of the structure and operation of the brain is important, as well as a willingness to examine metaphysical hypotheses, the paranormal and the spiritual. The brain, as we know from scientific research, has somewhere in the region of 100 billion neuron-connections. Each of these connections may form part of a memory. This leaves the memory with a capacity that is close to being infinite if storage is properly conducted and if it takes place in ideal circumstances.

The cortex plays a major role in processing sensory perception. However, research has shown that the prefrontal cortex does not become involved at all in sensory processing. These areas both left and right are involved in thinking. They play no part in sensory tasks. As we have seen each of the five senses sends messages to specific lobes in the brain where sense is made of the sensation received. The prefrontal cortex "is the only part that is free from the constant labour of sensory processing. It does not concern itself with the mundane tasks in life such as walking around, driving a car, making a cup of coffee or taking in the sensory perceptions from an unremarkable environment. All these can be done adequately without calling on the prefrontal cortex. So long as our mind is in neutral the prefrontal cortex merely ticks over. When something untoward occurs, however, or when we actually think rather than daydream the prefrontal cortex springs into life and we are jettisoned into full consciousness as from a tunnel into blazing sunshine."[7]

Creativity and planning are conducted in the prefrontal cortex. This is the centre of self-consciousness. In assessing the skills and acquired capabilities of a person we are assessing observable traits. The operations of the frontal lobes are not so easily assessed. The frontal lobes involve not only making sense of sensations acquired through the five senses but activating, directing and controlling the five senses. As well as making sense of information received through the senses, the frontal lobes analyse and devise plans and ideas based on that information. I can subsequently communicate those plans and ideas to others.

Consider the case of a person losing the use of the five senses but retaining the use of the frontal lobes. In that case no one would think of cutting off a life support machine. There is a chance that the senses would start to function again. But no matter how well the senses perform, without the analysing and creative ability of the frontal lobes, the information is of little value. This would seem to indicate that the frontal lobes constitute human intelligence. This section of the brain might therefore be considered as the mind. However, if we never had the use of the five senses but had perfect frontal lobes we may have nothing to think about, to plan or to analyse.

This conclusion is in line with St. Thomas Aquinas's statement: *Nihil in intellectu quod prius non feurit insensu* (Summa Theologica la, 84.7), there is nothing in the mind that has not already come through the senses. Aquinas stressed the experiential nature of human knowledge "we would have no knowledge of the world were it not for our experience of things."[8]

The frontal lobes, composed of a material substance depend on the senses also of a material substance to absorb the material world. There is no room for a spiritual or mental dimension in this closed circuit. Does a separate mental circuit exist? If two circuits exist then in what way do both connect, and, do they separate at death? We know through empirical observations that the material body returns to the earth and is recycled after death. Where does the spiritual mind go? Could it be that the brain constitutes the mental dimension of the person?

This reasoning pertains to the physical world. The brain is a material substance and we are referring to the acquisition of information on the material world and the analysis of that information. The unconscious mind may not be restricted by temporal or spatial boundaries. But as an individual human being I am placed in existential context relative to my position in time and space. My physical being is restricted by this relativity. The mind may not be so restricted.

Rene Descartes, the renowned French philosopher of the seventeenth century started his philosophy with the proposition that there is no certainty about anything, perhaps nothing exists, we cannot prove the existence of things.[9] From that point of departure he reasoned and set about proving that there is one certainty; ***I think***. Even doubting my existence is to think. This thinking proves my existence (my thinking existence) Thinking takes place in the frontal lobes of the brain. Could we then substitute Descartes' I think therefore I am with *I think, therefore I am my frontal lobes, or my frontal lobes think, therefore I am?* Could we take the mind to be a combination of all brain functioning? If so we could perhaps substitute the thinking person with the human brain and the senses. I could then say; *my brain and senses think*, therefore I am. This would equate the person's physical, material body with the human mind.

The brain is composed of a material substance, just like the rest of the body. Could I say, my foot feels pain, therefore I am? That would not prove my existence. The pain in my foot could be illusory. We know that phantom limb sensation affects more than half of those who undergo limb amputations. My foot is not ***me.*** I could exist without my foot. The 'I', as a thinking being, is quite different to a part of my material body, finger, foot, brain or any other part. *I think, therefore I am* involves abstract reasoning. It is not based on material substance, and it does not prove the existence of the material body or material substance of any kind. It just proves the existence of a thinking being.

A person's thinking ability and that person's ability to use language may be one and the same thing. Vigotsky held the view that thought is brought forth in words and a thought that has not been embodied in words remains a shadow. "Words play a central part, not only in the development of thought but in consciousness as a whole."[10] Ludwig Wittgenstein[11] the distinguished and renowned philosopher of language of the twentieth century, took language to be the principal defining aspect of the person. We are what we think and we think through language. I am a creature of language. Language is the distinguishing characteristic that makes us human. It is language that sets us apart from all other creatures on the earth.

The unparalleled development of the human prefrontal cortex brought speech and language, as a means of communication, to the fore. This gave humans a distinct advantage in the world. The initial use of gestures to communicate was gradually replaced by words. As we have noted, the areas of the brain that deal specifically with language are centred in the frontal and temporal lobes. In an educational context this knowledge of how the brain functions necessitates that we teach children in ways that will not go against the natural operation of the brain.

In the language regions of the brain, "stored impressions from different senses especially touch and hearing are brought together and reassembled into coherent memories."[12] Two areas that deal with language have been identified by the brain scientists Wernicke and Broca. Wernicke's area deals with comprehension. Broca's area is concerned with speech, articulation and syntax. Speech problems occur if Broca's area is damaged. If Wernicke's area only is damaged the victim may retain fluent speech, and, grammatical construction is unaffected, but what the victim says is nonsense. Serious damage to the connections between these two areas may leave the person unable to repeat what s/he hears. This is because the verbal language received and comprehended in Wernicke's area cannot be passed on to Broca's area for articulation.

With normal maturation Wernicke's area of the brain (the comprehension area) develops prior to Broca's area (the speech area). Because of the delay in speech development due to this maturation differential, the child can become frustrated in being unable to put words on his/her thoughts. This happens because the child understands more than s/he is able to articulate. Parents, teachers and child-care workers should be aware of this. A child may throw a tantrum, sulk or become very stubborn in frustration because s/he is unable to articulate his/her thoughts and feelings. Parents and teachers must spend time getting to know a child. They must observe the child's body language. If a child says, **Mammy you are not listening to me,** the parent must take heed. During the early school years, in particular, teachers ought to spend time talking with each individual child, questioning, listening, responding to, and eliciting a response from them.

With the development of speech and language comprehension the neurons in the prefrontal lobes begin to connect and communicate. Self-consciousness commences at this stage of development. "This self-consciousness suggests the emergence of an internal executor, the 'I' that most people say they feel inside their heads."[13] Neuroscience explains or defines the **mind** in this way. It sees the origin of the mind as the myelinization of neurons in the prefrontal lobes. In this way the mind is created by the brain. Bruce Hood, director of the Bristol Cognitive Development Centre in the Experimental Psychology Department at the University of Bristol claims that: "The mind has no real existence substantiated in the physical world. Psychology is the scientific study of the mind, but the mind does not exist in any material sense. Rather, the mind is the natural operating system that runs on the input and output of the brain's activity. We can study its operations, but we would be wrong to think that the mind occupies a material existence independently of the brain"[14]

The development of the human brain has occurred much more rapidly than it has with any other creature on earth. This has caused no great consternation. The accepted belief is that human evolution accounts for this and there is no mystery about it. It is true that the human brain has evolved with gigantic leaps in comparison with all other animals and it continues to develop at a disproportionate rate to all other creatures on earth. Attempts to establish limits to human intelligence have failed. The child who is weak academically in early childhood years may produce masterpieces in art, music, literature and poetry in later life with what appears to be limited intelligence. In contrast, the apparently gifted child may fail to achieve in adulthood what we expected or predicted of him/her as a child.

The bodily functioning of all creatures stems from brain activity. For the human being speech, skilled movement, hearing, sight and sight recognition, as well as the emotions and general behaviour, reside in specific and identifiable areas of the brain. From this information it would appear that intelligence can only be defined in terms of brain activity. We know that a person needs more than legs in order to win a race or even to run at all. Yet without legs it would be a major task for a person to run. Likewise a person needs more than eyes to see, but can one see without eyes?

As medical science advances we will find that in the future, it may be possible for someone to run without legs. Artificial limbs may do the running for the person. In the future, too, eye transplants or perhaps artificial eyes may be able to perform the function of the eyes. Without the brain, however, we know that the eyes cannot recognise or make sense of what is seen. Without the power of the brain, the legs, or artificial limbs cannot move. Hence, it would seem that the brain is not only the driving force of the person but to all intents and purposes it is the person. The more we study the anatomy, physiology and operations of the brain the more we may come to believe that it is the brain that directs the person and therefore that the brain is the mind.

This belief that the brain is the mind appears to be further confirmed by an experiment carried out by Guang Yue and quoted by Alistair Smith in *THE BRAINS BEHIND IT*: "In November 2001 Guang Yue, an exercise physiologist at the Cleveland Clinic Foundation in Ohio, published findings suggesting that you could strengthen muscles just by imagining yourself exercising - - - this offers benefits to those recovering from an injury or a stroke and who might be too weak to go straight back to physical activity. Guang Yue and his team asked ten volunteers to imagine flexing their biceps as hard as they could for as long as they could during imaginary training sessions for five days each week. Their brain activity was recorded and so was electrical activity at the motor neurons of the arm muscles. The training lasted three months. After the first two weeks the participants showed an amazing 13.5% increase in upper arm strength and they maintained this until the training stopped."[15]

To deduce from the above experiment that essentially the person is the brain would be an unjustified deduction. Guang Yue's experiment might be interpreted differently. Perhaps the mind controls and directs the brain. The mind instructs and causes the brain to exercise control over the senses and other bodily functioning. The unconscious mind can influence the physical environment. It operates with greater effectiveness when the brain and senses are dormant.

What or where is the mind? Could it be a waste of time inquiring into the composition of the human mind if it cannot be empirically scrutinised. In this scientific age we are reluctant to accept anything that is not quantifiable. However, we may have to accept that the mind is outside the range of any type of empirical measuring device. We can inquire into the material aspect of the person and into the nature of the material world. At the end of that inquiry we will still be left with the inquirer. A philosophical investigation into the nature of the human being ought to examine the subject as well as the object in that investigation. In fact the subject should be the focal point of such a philosophical inquiry. The object, the material aspect of the person, is mainly a matter for scientific investigation. We must also inquire into the relationship between the subject and the object. The growth and development of science has placed a disproportionate emphasis on empirical research compared to philosophical investigation. This shift of emphasis has detrimentally affected philosophical reasoning. Proportional balance may need to be restored between those two areas of study.

Before proceeding further we will look briefly at the origin of two schools of thought **Rationalism** and **Materialism** and establish to what extent one or other can give us an insight into an understanding of the human mind. Both philosophies can be traced back to the ancient Greek thinkers, the period 500 BC. Parmenides and Heraclitus were Rationalists, Democritus was a Materialist. Parmenides did not believe that our senses were capable of giving us an accurate and true picture of the world. He believed that human reason is the primary source of all knowledge. An absolute belief in the primacy of human reason is known as Rationalism. Heraclitus, a contemporary of Parmenides, had a certain amount of faith in what we perceive. He believed that everything is in a constant state of flux, nothing is permanent. We cannot step into the same river twice. The second time we step into the river all the original water will have moved on. Contemporary rationalism holds that human reason is the primary source of all knowledge and that human thinking is constantly evolving. It is unpredictable. It is inventive, calculating and creative. It is constantly changing, never static.

Democritus, on the other hand, didn't believe in a soul or a spirit that could influence or interfere with the natural law. All that exists, according to him, are atoms and nothingness. He believed only in material substance. His description of the soul was of something composed of soul atoms. At death those soul atoms disperse in all directions. It is possible for them to become part of another soul. But the human being, according to Democritus, has no immortal soul. This is in line with contemporary Materialist thinking. Karl Marx might be seen as the father of contemporary atheistic materialism. The material requirements of society were Marx's preoccupation. However, he did not see the mind as passive in the material world as was the case in the pure empiricist tradition. He maintained that the subject and the object of experience are in a continual adapting process. We must direct our experience purposively in order to ensure our survival. This appears to assume the existence of a mind that can purposively direct experience rather than nature directing itself.

Marx's philosophy proposed that the spiritual needs of the person, which dominated thinking in the civilized world up to then, be replaced by the promotion of people's material needs. Spiritual leaders were not putting their preaching into practice. They preached the Christian message that 'man does not live on bread alone' but lived in luxury themselves. They saw the poor as the salt of the earth because it was their poverty that allowed the rich to remain wealthy. Marx maintained that religion was a drug that kept people sedated and prevented them from thinking. His phrase was: 'Religion is the opium of the people.' The fear of hell and promise of a heaven after death were powerful motivating threats and incentives. His atheistic materialism encouraged the proletariat to shed fears of an afterlife in hell and replace that fear with the joy of sharing in the earth's wealth in this life. There is no room for a spiritual dimension or a separation of mind and body in this philosophy. The brain and the mind are one and the same thing in the view of contemporary materialists.

Different religions have various views about what happens to the soul after the death of the body. It goes to heaven or to some other extra terrestrial place. The soul dies with the body. The soul enters another human being or animal after the death of the body. These are among the beliefs concerning the soul's destiny promulgated by different religious leaders, cults, or societies.

The most prevalent viewpoint in contemporary atheistic societies is that the concepts of a God, a soul or a spirit are illusory, mythical and unrealistic. The soul or mind is a Ghost and does not have a real existence. The concept of the soul originated in prehistoric times and has lived on in the consciousness of humans down through the ages. There is no logical basis for accepting the reality of the soul. This viewpoint emanates from a scientific/empiricist culture. It permeates and pervades contemporary materialist thinking.

It may not be quite so easy to dismiss or obliterate the concept of the soul. Perhaps it is the soul that is the defining aspect of the person. In our everyday use of language, we say: *I think, or, I use my brain to think*, **not**, my brain thinks, or, my brain uses me to think. This sentence gives the mind a precedence and superiority over the brain.' I' am the subject. ***My brain*** is the object.

At a time in history when rationalism and spiritualism dominated the world materialism emerged, blossomed and flourished. Today as materialism dominates rationalism and spiritualism may re-emerge to establish a new dawn in human thinking. However, before we attempt to make any assumption about the essence of the human mind, we will need to analyze the relationship between human intelligence and a person's behaviour, character and personality.

ENDNOTES:

CHAPTER I

[1] de Bono, Edward **WHY SO STUPID?** How the human race has never learned to think Published by Blackhall publishing, Blackrock, Dublin, 2006 p.3

[2] Ryle, Gilbert **THE CONCEPT OF MIND** Published by Hutchinson, London 1949

[3] Darwin, Charles **THE ORIGIN OF SPECIES** First published 1859

[4] Planet Gliese 581C discovered 2007

[5] Nietzsche, F **THE WILL TO POWER** – translated by W. Kaufmann & R.J. Hollingdale Edited with commentary by Walter Kaufmann – published by Weidenfeld Nicolson, London 1967

[6] Smith, Alistair **THE BRAINS BEHIND IT** Published by Network Educational Press Ltd Stafford – revised edition 2004 p.36

[7] Carter, Rita– **MAPPING THE MIND** - First published in Great Britain 1998, 4th Impression 2004 p. 299; Weidenfeld & Nicolson, paperback edition by Phoenix 2000 p.36

[8] Copleston, F.C. **AQUINAS** - Penguin books – Harmondsworth 1963 Pp. 25-28

[9] Descartes, Rene **DISCOURSE ON METHOD; THE MEDITATIONS** Rules for the Direction of the mind – translated by L.J. Lafleur N.Y.& Indianapolis. The Liberal Arts Press 1950 and The Bobbs-Merrill Co., Inc.1961

[10] Vigotsky, L.S. *Thought and Speech,* in **PSYCHOLINGUISTICS** *A book of readings; -* Ed. by Sol Spaorta. Publ. Holt, Rinehart & Winston. N.Y., Chicago, London 1961 p.534

[11] Wittgenstein, Ludwig **TRACTATUS LOGICO-PHILOSOPHICUS**, First German edition 1921. English translation by D. F. Pears and B. F. Mc Guinness, Routledge and Keegan Paul

[12] Carter, Rita **MAPPING THE MIND,** op. cit. p.228

[13] Ibid p.22

[14] Hood, Bruce **SUPERSENSE -** From Superstition to Religion Publisher, Harper Collins 2009 p.147

[15] Smith, Alistair **THE BRAINS BEHIND IT** op. cit. p. 11

CHAPTER II

COGITO, ERGO SUM, & SCIENCE
Language and thinking

Cogito, ergo sum, ergo, sum res cogitans – (I think, therefore I am, therefore, I am a thinking being). From this logical reasoning of Rene Descartes I can conclude that I am a being with language. Recorded language is a verifiable concrete manifestation of the thinking process and is the bridge that spans the mental and the material worlds. In stating orally or in writing: *Cogito ergo sum*, I am materialising a thought. I am making concrete an idea. If I have doubts about my existence then I am thinking.

"Descartes does admit that his insight is also expressible by, '*dubito, ergo, sum*'"[1] (I doubt, therefore, I am). To doubt is to think. If I doubt that something exists, I am thinking about it, or, about its non existence.

Does the essence of the human person consist solely of thinking? The majority of today's philosophers and scientists do not believe that this is the case. "The verb cogitare (to think) was traditionally very wide."[2] It contained in its meaning such acts of consciousness as; judging, sensing, willing and feeling. Descartes was right in pointing out that no matter what else is included in the essence of the human being thinking is the primary element.

Many philosophers coming after Descartes have refused to accept the supremacy of the mind over the body. From the Scientific perspective there can be no separation of mind and body. "Humans are conscious automata. Our bodies generate our minds."[3] Descartes' meaning of existence was different to Empiricists' understanding of the concept. Empiricists see existence as something that can be grasped by the senses, something that is sensible (observable, tangible etc.) and quantifiable. There is a difference between the intellectual world and the material world, a difference that has been recognised since our earliest records of human reasoning. The mind is not composed of material substance. Science cannot explain the mind through an examination of the physical body.

With the unprecedented development of science and technology in the 20th century, the material dimension of the person came more into focus. Material advances have benefited the human body. Inventions and discoveries of new drugs, and anaesthetics have helped to ease pain and prolong life. The twentieth century could be deemed the century of science and information technology. Humans, with the aid of science, have invented aeroplanes and spacecraft to conquer the skies and explore outer space.

Medical science has introduced heart, lung, kidney and liver transplants as well as keyhole surgery, chemotherapy, radium and laser treatments for many diseases, injuries and deformities. Motors and batteries have been invented to drive and power cars, buses, ships, aircraft carriers, spacecraft, trains, cranes and bulldozers. The invention of electricity has mollified the chores of domestic living. Automatic washing machines, dishwashers, electric kettles, microwave ovens, cookers, refrigerators and freezers have made home life easier for many people. Information technology has seen the development of television, video players / recorders, mobile phones, the facsimile, computer and e-mail. A person can communicate with another in almost any part of the globe by pressing a few buttons on a phone hand set or on a computer keyboard.

In contemporary times any attempt to define or explain the mind, the universe or the thinking process outside the realm of science, is seen as naïve and non-sense. Scientists maintain that they will find the answer to a full understanding of the person in due course. Biology, psychology, linguistics, psycholinguistics, neurolinguistics will find an explanation to the thinking process. The mystery of the mind and language will be removed. New discoveries and inventions challenge the traditional role of philosophy in seeking to understand the mind.

This is a misconceived notion. To date none of the developed sciences has given us any reason to believe that a definition of intelligence is imminent. Philosophy continues the search for an understanding of the mind and to expose weaknesses in scientific attempts to achieve an empirical verification of human intelligence. Science cannot measure thinking, the person's capacity to choose or assess one's responsibility levels. Neither can science measure an individual's powers of creativity and imagination. We can recognise those qualities in people. Many people possess tremendous creative and imaginative powers but they may not display them or may not be given the opportunity to put them into practice. The malnourished child in the third world will hardly have many opportunities to invent and create. We contemplate measurement of those qualities in the affluent world only, and even here, those measurements are often no more than a means of screening people for some sinister purpose, capital gain being the principal motivating factor.

Science may try to explain spirituality through demonstrable experiments and factual information on brain functioning. Most religions propagate the belief that a supreme being created the mental/spiritual dimension of the person. Philosophy endeavours to explain the supernatural through metaphysics, first principles, cause and effect and language analysis. Many contemporary philosophers tend to dismiss the notion of a supreme being. They attribute more credence to science than did their predecessors.

In the future, psycho-linguistics may explain some of the mechanisms involved in the thinking process, particularly in the area of communication. Genetic science may advance to the stage of being able to construct or reconstruct a person, but another human being will be a part of the reconstruction and that reconstruction will have to be carried out, not by science, but, by a scientist, a human being. We must rely on a human mind in order to arrive at an understanding of the human mind. This is a logical conclusion for even if a machine could measure and determine the capability of the thinking person the results would have to be received and analysed by another thinking being, otherwise they would remain at the material level. They would be no more than data accumulated by a machine for a machine. It is the scientist whom we have under the microscope here and not the science.

We can dismiss the notion that science will explain everything. An invention is not greater than the inventor. Science is a human invention designed to test and explain the constitution and composition of all animate and inanimate beings including human existence in the universe, Science without a scientist would be like a whirlpool in a river without water. The human's craving to understand the universe springs from a craving to understand him / herself. Why would a person want to inquire into, and understand anything if it did not relate to the inquirer seeking the answer. We are born with a desire to understand, explore, invent and create. We are born too, with a craving to find an explanation for the universe, and, a meaning for human existence.

Science cannot define the human mind so we must look to the scientist. Given time, science, through a scientist, will dispel many of the myths about the person. But a comprehensive explanation of the mind will remain outside the scope of science. Even when all the myths are dispelled, the mind will still be elusive. The scientist, as a person, will stand outside and above the science. The scientist will continue to be the person in the laboratory seeking to put gig-saw pieces together. Each discovery may open up a whole new gig-saw puzzle. It will give us a better understanding of the universe but may not offer any better insight into the thinking existential human mind.

Philosophers who adopt a holistic approach to an understanding of the person refuse to accept a separation of mind and body. They do not want to separate the thinking mind from the physical body. There are those who maintain that I am an intellectual being with a body and others who see it the other way round, I am a physical being that thinks. It would seem that no matter how much time we spend trying to tease out and to understand the mind, we will always return to the unsettled question: is everything in the world composed of two realities, *spirit* and *matter*, or, is there but one substance?

The history of philosophy throws up numerous arguments to support each of those viewpoints. Spinoza[4] maintained that the dualistic theory of the world postulated by Descartes is nonsense. For him everything can be reduced to just one single *substance*. Nature controls everything according to Spinoza. What we call thought and extension, mind and matter are just different aspects of how nature manifests itself. Spinoza believed that I do not control everything that happens in my body neither do I choose my thinking. Nature decides those things. The individual person has no free will. If we can come to realize and accept that everything happens naturally then we can achieve an intuitive understanding of the workings of nature. Spinoza maintained that states of mind are just names for the appetites that vary according to the mood or state of the body at a particular time.

John Locke and David Hume, eighteenth century British empiricist philosophers, maintained that there is nothing in the mind that has not entered through the senses. According to Locke the mind is a '*tabula rasa*' (a clean slate) at birth. All thoughts and ideas result from sense experiences. In A Treatise of Human Nature, David Hume questioned Descartes' thesis and particularly one of the deductions from his original thesis: Descartes having established his own existence through his thinking then went on to claim that anything of which a person has a clear and distinct idea exists. From this he deduced that since he had, a clear and distinct idea of God in his mind, God therefore exists. Hume rejected Descartes' conclusion.

According to David Hume if God is a being who is infinitely wise, infinitely intelligent and infinitely good and just, we must understand the meaning of wisdom, intelligence, goodness and justice and we come to that understanding from experience in the world, acquired through the senses. George Berkeley[6] an Irish philosopher of the same period, maintained that the spiritual dimension of the person is superior to the material. He went to the other extreme and questioned the reality of the physical world. Berkeley maintained that nothing exists other than what we perceive - *esse est percipi* (to be is to be perceived). We may sense tangible or sensible objects but we cannot perceive their underlying essence. I cannot perceive what I do not see, feel, touch, taste or smell. We can perceive only ideas and it is unreasonable to presume that there is a material substance behind our perceptions, according to Berkeley. He was an Idealist, He believed only in the reality of ideas.

George Berkeley held the view that the existence of God is far more perceptible than the existence of the material world. He questioned the notions of time and space. Things in the world around us may be just figments of our imagination. We might be living in a dream world with regard to time and space. Time to us is not as it is to God. Ironically, Berkeley's view of our intuitive awareness of God is not too far removed from the view held by Spinoza i.e. that we have an intuitive understanding of things. However, they differed fundamentally in that Spinoza believed that Nature directs and controls the universe while Berkeley believed that it is God that directs and controls everything.

Idealism found another adversary in phenomenology. Edmund Husserl[7] in establishing phenomenology as a philosophy started by suspending judgement on the reality of things. Phenomenology accepts the existence of phenomena as the only true reality. That which we can touch, see, smell, taste and hear is real. Descartes began by doubting the existence of everything. Husserl started by saying; let's begin by holding that nothing has a reality beyond what we sense. Husserl never got beyond the phenomena. He could never show or prove that anything is other than *the phenomena*. Even if an object has an essence we cannot sense it. An essence is not real; it is an abstraction. Phenomenology gives the senses and sense experience an unwarranted priority over the mind and mental processing. Ironically, it is the mind that thinks in this way and it is mental processing that draws conclusions from premises. But conclusions from premises have meaning only if the premises are true.

From the two extreme philosophies Empiricism and Idealism emerged Realism.

Idealists maintain that nothing can be known except thoughts: everything that we know is in the mind. According to empiricists that which we sense is the only reality. Bertrand Russell, a British philosopher of the twentieth century, sought to bridge the gap between those two extreme philosophies and aimed to establish realism as an acceptable alternative: "Realism maintains …. that … we know objects directly, in sensation certainly, and perhaps also in memory and thought."[8]

Existentialism is another philosophy that emerged and flourished in the twentieth century. It focused attention on human consciousness as it operates in the material world. Existentialism is concerned with the plight of the person as s/he lives in the world and makes everyday decisions. Those decisions make that person what s/he is. Jean Paul Sartre[9] a French existentialist philosopher, emphasised the uniqueness of human existence and how it differs from all other animate and inanimate beings. We create our essence through decisions we make from choices presented to us in life. Sartre maintained that a person cannot be defined till after death. He is correct in the sense that the 'I' (me) of today can change radically tomorrow in appearance, in character, in knowledge acquired and in experiences gained.

Existentialist philosophers take the view that the definition of the person is to be found in what s/he does, believes, says and thinks. We cannot fully define a person until after s/he has died. After death we can define the person in terms of what s/he has achieved in life. Till that point the person does not have an essence only an existence. It is the person's existence, what that individual chooses and does as s/he exists in the world that will ultimately, (at death) compose his/her essence.

The person while existing; i.e. acting, reacting, expressing thoughts, responding to ideas, creating, composing, carrying out responsibilities and choices that are part and partial of daily living is in the process of forming his/her essence. Existence precedes essence. Inanimate objects and all living creatures, except for humans, have an essence. We can define a stone, a television set or a tree. We can also define a dog, a shark or an eagle. All creatures will do as nature bids, nature controls everything. Humans are beings without an essence. We can make choices and defy the course of nature. A person can decide to leave a place or to live a different type of life. Existence, as living and experiencing, cannot be measured or defined. At one's death the sum total of a person's experiences and knowledge acquired in life, become that person's essence.

Martin Heidegger[10] also an existentialist thinker, saw death as the goal of life. He refers to our daily existence as a life facing death. After death one's works, thoughts and dreams can be charted. Death is the defining moment. We can define the person in terms of the actions and words that s/he has performed, uttered or written in life. However, we could say that that is only a definition of the individual's recorded or observable works, words and deeds. Existentialism views the person as a living mind and since each individual is unpredictable in thoughts and actions we cannot give a definition of a living person.

Those varied and diverse philosophies are all attempting to understand the mind and the thinking process, and, how humans comprehend, interact with, and relate to the world outside us. Out of this great diversity of philosophies emerged linguistics. Our ability to use language is unique. Philosophers of language are concerned primarily with the thinking dimension of the person. Ludwig Wittgenstein tried to take the mystery out of thinking in maintaining that we think through language. *The limits of my language mean the limits of my world.*[11] Noam Chomsky, a contemporary linguistic philosopher does not accept that we are born with a blank slate, *a tabula rasa*. He maintains that we are born with a predisposition to language, with: "deep and restrictive principles that determine the nature of human language and are rooted in the specific character of the human mind."[12] We are like pre-strung instruments, he maintains, all the cords and notes are there already. We just need to learn to play them.

There is little doubt about our being born with a predilection to learn language. The foetus in the womb can hear sounds in the outside world. The sounds s/he hears most frequently are speech sounds. The speech sounds that hold most relevance are those of the mother, in the first instance, followed by the voices of the mother's closest and most intimate associates, her husband, partner, friends, relatives, companions and other siblings. The foetus absorbs highly charged language, mainly. This is because of the energy exerted in expressing it. Swear words are picked up and unmistakably deciphered and understood. Words expressing feelings are more readily understood than non-emotive, neutral words. Strong, expressive, highly charged language; exclamations, nervous intonation and deliberately controlled speech as well as grammatical construction of speech sounds are what the foetus attends to mostly during the relaxed gestation period. In living situations too, one learns best while in an uninterrupted, relaxed state. It is not surprising then that rules of language as well as a great deal of other characteristics learned in the womb emerge with the baby at birth.

It is important that educators and parents not only attend to the education of the child from the time of birth to five years of age and in preschool, but, also at the prenatal stage. Parents ought to be aware of, and appreciate their unparalleled power and responsibility in education at the prenatal stage. Expectant mothers should endeavour to avoid stress. They should consume nutritious foods. These measures will have affects on the future health and well being of the child. Speaking to the foetus in the womb, in positive reassuring terms, playing soft and relaxing music, and displaying a *positive attitude during the pregnancy ought to be encouraged.*

However, it would be tragic if prenatal education set about producing robot-like individuals. Prenatal education ought to aim at developing relaxation, self-esteem, positive thinking as well as appreciation of the arts; music drama, dance, visual art etc. Clear, unambiguous voice recordings might be developed that would give all prenatal children a fair and equal opportunity from the start. *The prenatal child should not be bombarded with learning structures. On the contrary, relaxation, music and rhythmic sounds should be encouraged so that the child is born with the proclivity to relax and be in harmony with nature. This could prepare the person to set aside time to relax in order to allow the mind to create, invent and discover free from outside interference, as s/he progresses through life.* We have an obligation to assist in human evolution and it is the mind that is most capable of that task. The mind must be allowed time and space to assess and analyse evolutionary processes as well as to evaluate and make decision on one's own destiny.

Perhaps the mind of the foetus in the womb can give directions to the mother. She may believe that the direction is from nature and not from an intellect. While the world impinges on the mind of the unborn that mind may be able to accept or reject what is perceived. It is important for expectant mothers and all prenatal care workers, nurses and doctors to realise that the baby in the womb is capable of receiving and accepting suggestions and instructions. Because the baby in the womb is relaxed s/he is easily influenced. The mind of the foetus may be imaginative and creative. Much more research is required to establish the learning potential of the mind in the womb.

In the future, society may see a need to employ teachers to redress the harmful influences on the mind of the unborn child of a drug or alcohol addicted mother or mother's partner. Stress from pressures in the workplace, from society generally or from family disputes and altercations may have an adverse effect on the unborn child. At no other time in life will that human mind be so receptive to positive educational suggestions and with minimal distractions. The opportunity to allow the mind of the unborn to relax, create, learn and develop valuable caring traits should not be missed.

Existentialists claim that I am the author of my own destiny. This is not fully correct, any more than Spinoza's claim that nature controls me and I have no free will. There are influences outside my control that may force me to choose other than the way I would like to choose. However, I need not succumb to the pressure. I can resist outside pressures and choose my own course in life. To say that I know the world through appearances is valid for it is through observation, empirical examination and scientific inquiry that I come to know the world. But there is some mystical aspect about the person that requires further examination. The suggestion that we think in language seems correct and to maintain that we are born with a predilection to language appears to be true too. Yet as separate theories neither of them explains or defines the mind of the person.

From *Cogito, ergo sum* Descartes concluded, *ergo, sum res cogitans* (therefore I am a thinking being). The material / physical body dimension is missing from this reasoning. While *Cogito, ergo sum* could also apply to spirits we don't know for certain that spirits exist. I do know that I exist and as we have noted even to doubt this is to think. I can also actualize and record my thinking through speech, writings and in art forms. I know that others can do likewise because I can bear witness to their speech, writing and art works. I can communicate my thoughts to others and they can communicate their thoughts to me through speech, art, drama, architecture, music etc. We cannot communicate in this way with spirits. Contemplatives, through meditation may be able to do so. We cannot verify this. I can have many beliefs that appear self-evident to me but unless I can empirically verify them they will be treated with scepticism in this scientific age. Beliefs do not necessarily belong to the material world. The formation and subsequent acceptance of some beliefs are formed independently of the senses.

Descartes' neglect of the material dimension of the person has been, not balanced, but, far outweighed, by the physical sciences' neglect of the mental dimension. Contemporary materialism assumes an overwhelming dominance over the Cartesian mind. Scientific research is crucial in trying to understand the human being and the universe in which we live. It is most important to dispel myths and to verify or falsify speculative theories. In contemporary times philosophy is often castigated and viewed as mere theory and idle speculation. Today, instead of giving any credence to Descartes' *cogito, ergo sum*, it is the material body, the aspect of the individual neglected by Descartes that is celebrated.

We may need to examine in greater detail the evolution of the human thinking process. It seems clear that no single area of the brain can fully account for thinking, any more than an athlete's legs alone can account for his or her winning a race. We accept that a person's running ability depends mainly on the strength and fitness of the leg muscles and rowing ability depends mainly on the power and fitness of the arm and chest muscles. All animals possess those abilities, many at a much higher level than humans. However, long term planning and general reasoning powers reside mainly in the frontal lobes of the brain. Consequently, brain scientists must place greater emphasis on, and conduct much more in-depth research into the frontal lobes where logical reasoning, planning and creativity occur.

When scientists push their experiments to the limit, however, they will discover that neither the frontal lobes nor the brain in its totality can account fully for human thinking. It is accepted that I use only a small fraction of my brain during my lifetime and in my everyday living. We spend a lot of time daydreaming. There is a *Practical Philosophy* that encourages us to live each moment to the full and to concentrate and focus at all times on what we are doing. But, as humans with physical bodies, it is not possible to live in this way. The brain is unable to remain fully active, alert and attentive all the time. The brain needs periodic rests from concentration. In that restful state the mind, (the unconscious mind), assumes control. It organises and categorises events experienced, and, information acquired. If we never had time to daydream we would act, live and behave in the animal state. It is in daydreaming that we often create and develop the most elevated and sophisticated ideas and plans. Creating and planning usually spring from the unconscious mind.

Language usage, memory storage and recall, imagination, creativity and our ability to plan are the characteristics that elevate us above the level of other animals. These distinguishing human characteristics reside and operate in the frontal lobes of the brain. This gives the frontal lobes a crucial role in the life of humans. Yet these lobes form only one aspect of human life albeit a very important aspect, their operation is essential in language communication.

Ludwig Wittgenstein maintained that thinking and language are identical. Language is the vehicle of thought. Oral and written language demonstrate empirically the thinking process. Thinking is manifested in works of art, architecture, literature, music, engineering achievements and technological innovations and inventions. Language is thinking if we accept that that which cannot be said cannot be thought.

Language is a uniquely human characteristic. The poet, writer, sculpture, musician, painter, engineer and scientist create their works through language. When a person thinks, that person does not have meanings going through his/her mind distinct from the language in which the thinking and the ideas are expressed.

Wittgenstein did not view words as a central part of the development of thought but as thoughts … words are units of thought. Yet using phrases like 'language embodies thought' seems to imply that, *there are thoughts* and *there is the wrapping,* that wrapping is the language. When we use phrases such as: *I thought of the word, I am searching for the word,* or, *can you think of the sentence?* We are not separating thought and language. We are separating thought and verbal expressions. We are distinguishing between ideas and the articulation of ideas. We may need to think of a word to express an idea. I could have an idea but am unable to put words on that idea.

Wittgenstein often repeated the phrase *language in use* by which he meant that there is no need to look beyond the language we use in order to seek the thoughts it represents. What we accept as common everyday language should be accepted as common everyday thinking. Language in use expresses the thoughts and ideas in circulation at the time of expression. Language is not simply the outward expression of thoughts. We think through language. The limits of my language are the limits of my thoughts and the limits of my thoughts are the limits of my world.

Wittgenstein did not suggest that the limits of my sense experiences as the limits of my world. The origin of some thoughts may not have come from the senses. If this is so then where do they come from? We might also ask if the limits of my language are the limits of my world then is that world potentially infinite. While there may be a finite number of concepts in any written or spoken language the permutations and combinations of those concepts, and the words or symbols that express them is enormous but is finite nevertheless. However, since each human being is capable of creating new symbols of thought, words, then even one new word, through permutations and combinations, can vastly increase the limits of a person's world. There is no limit to the amount of words or concepts that one can create. We may have thoughts that do not pertain to the material world.

When we learn a language, words and concepts, we are learning thoughts and ideas, the thoughts of contemporary society. We are also learning the thoughts and ideas of our immediate predecessors and of our earlier ancestors. When we create a new word we are creating an original thought. We can conceive new ideas too. They may be simple or complex. We then make concrete those ideas in expressive language form. This process appears to give thought a priority over language. This is because we tend to view language in terms of oral or written words, sentences and expressions and not as a conceptualising process.

In the pragmatic world of everyday existence we learn a language and in that learning we come into contact with ideas, thoughts and concepts. This is what constitutes the extent and the limits of my world. What my body and my brain are capable of doing represent the power of the machine and we appear to be limited in the everyday practical world by that machine. We must now ask; from where have all the great ideas and innovations come? They have not come from the everyday language that we learn but mainly from introspection, meditation and inspiration. The machine, like any machine in the world of physics, is very limited. A machine is capable of doing what it is designed to do and no more. Human intelligence is different. It is not limited, as a machine is limited. It is limitless.

The reason I say *my head is sore,* or, *my leg hurts me* is because I realize that my head and my leg are not me but they affect me. When I say, 'I *caught myself warming myself in front of the fire'* [13] I give the impression that there is more than one of me there. This kind of language, as Gilbert Ryle points out, seems to suggest that there is a whole battery of 'me s' within me. This, of course, is utter nonsense. If we analyse the language we use it becomes clear that there is only one **me.** If we put too much emphasis on analysing words and sentence structure we can become embroiled in pedantic nonsense. That is no better than sophistry, arguing for the sake of arguing.

In this type of philosophical meandering we can lose the meaning of the utterance.

When I say *I hurt my leg* it is quite clear that my leg is not **me** but is simply possessed by me. It is my leg not your leg, but it is just a leg. It could even be your leg that is hurting me. When I say 'I caught myself warming myself in front of the fire', the 'I' is **me,** and, the first *myself* is **me** or 'I' in reflection. The second myself is *my body.* We do not need to try to complicate the structure of the language. It is the meaning that matters. The meaning is often clearer than the structure. The structure is the making concrete of the idea. We might compare this process to a building structure. The plan is formed in a mind then it is articulated in oral or written language and in diagram form. Finally, it is made concrete in brick, steel, wood or some synthetic substance or a combination of all those materials.

If I say *I realised that I was sitting on the wall.* The first 'I' is the intellectual thinking 'I' that reflects. The second 'I' refers to my body though it also includes the thinking 'I'. If I changed the sentence *to: I realised that my body was sitting on the wall,* I would not have radically changed the meaning of the sentence though it lacks the completeness of the original sentence. I use 'I' in the second place just to confirm that I am in control of my body at that moment. A split second later I may cease to realise that I am sitting on the wall, a friend may come along and we begin to talk about Rome. The realisation of my sitting on the wall fades from consciousness and may not return, even though I jump off the wall and pick up a coin that I notice on the ground in front of me and I then sit back on the wall again. During this time I am thinking about the Coliseum and the sun beaming down on me as I walk the streets of Rome.

If I say, *my leg hurts me,* it might appear, on a first reading that my leg is the subject but on reflection it is very clear that, my leg is the object. I am the subject. I feel pain. The leg is the cause of the pain. The leg may need assistance. I may have to seek help from a doctor or surgeon. The leg may need to be amputated to relieve the pain. *The loss of that wallet hurt me* is only accidentally different to, *that broken arm hurt me.* My car was stolen and burned is only accidentally different to my leg was burned and amputated. We can replace the car and we can replace the leg.

The suggestion that the mind is a Ghost in the machine is misleading. Ghosts are seen as figments of the imagination in much the same way as leprechauns and fairies are fictitious characters. The machine is seen as the authentic article. This is a naïve, materialist view of a human being. Expressive language did not develop to its present degree of sophistication without good reason. We did not invent or develop an expressive language in order to confuse ourselves and confuse others. There is no great ambiguity involved in the language we use every day. If we accept the validity of Wittgenstein's *language in use*, and, *language embodies thought* then our language is an expression of our evolutionary state at a particular time in history. I am not speaking of any particular spoken or written language for all languages use a similar semantic and syntactic structure. We tend to think of language in terms of verbal communication. We also have Braille, sign-language and body-language. We have the language of art, music, drama and architecture.

Why are we in search of a simplistic definition of the complex human being? Why did the human brain become so superior to the brains of all other animals? Perhaps up to a certain point in evolution we were preoccupied with caring for the body, ensuring survival and adapting the body to suit the environment as well as changing the environment to suit our needs.

The question of the origin of the mind may be the topic of discussion for another time. It raises the follow up question: can we determine the ultimate destiny of the mind? Descartes' definition of the mind, as that dimension of the person that is involved in thinking seems reasonable. The mind is the intellectual aspect of the person. It is the defining and differentiating dimension of the human being. We may be able to define the meaning and essence of intelligence but we cannot measure it. We must differentiate between definition and quantification. We can define infinity but we cannot quantify it.

The mind is always active. It is potency. Jean Paul Sartre was right in one sense in saying that the individual person cannot be defined till after death. In physical terms this is correct but the person's ideas and plans may continue to be put into effect long after death. Science cannot verify the non-existence of the mind or falsify its existence after the death of the body.

Many of today's scientists would like to be able to prove that human intelligence is rooted in the brain. They would like to establish too, that human intelligence is measurable. They want to establish an inseparable link between the mind and the material body. The vast majority of contemporary philosophers and scientists are reluctant to speak of the mind as having an existence outside the life of the body. This would allow the Ghost to return and become part of the definition of the person. We want to deny the existence of anything that is not quantifiable.

ENDNOTES:

CHAPTER II

[1] Hintikka, Jaakko *Cogito ergo sum; influence or performance* in **DESCARTES** *A collection of critical essays*, Ed. by Willis Doney p.123

[2] Ibid p.135

[3] Hood, Bruce, op.cit. p.148

[4] Spinoza, Baruch **THE CHIEF WORKS OF BENEDICT DE SPINOZA** (Brauch Spinoza) Trans. with introduction by R H.M. Elwes, printed in one Vol. N.Y. 1951

[5] Hume, David **A TREATISE OF HUMAN NATURE** Longmans, Green and Co London 1882

[6] Berkeley, George **PHILOSOPHICAL WRITINGS** - selected and edited by Jessop, T.E. London 1952. Greenwood press N.Y. 1969

[7] J.N. Mohanty and W.R.McKenna A textbook **HUSSERL'S PHENOMENOLOGY** 1989 pp 250-253

[8] Russell, B. **THE ANALYSIS OF MIND** London, G. Allen and Unwin Ltd. First published in. 1921 p.20

[9] Sartre, J.P **BEING AND NOTHINGNESS** Published by Methuen, London 1969

[10] Heidegger, Martin **BEING AND TIME** – Translated by Macquarrie, J. and Robinson, E. SCM press - London 1962

[11] Wittgenstein, Ludwig **TRACTATUS LOGICO - PHILOSOPHICUS** op.cit. p115 (5.6)

[12] Chomsky, Noam **LANGUAGE AND MIND** – Harcourt Brace Jovanovich 1968 Inc. N.Y., Chicago, San Francisco, Atlanta – reprinted 1972 p.102

[13] Ryle, Gilbert **THE CONCEPT OF MIND** op.cit. pp.189, 190

CHAPTER III

HISTORICITY & PERSONALITY
The unconscious mind

Historicity views the mind in the context of the flow of history. Thoughts are passed down from generation to generation. We are products of history. Yet we have free will and, to a large extent, we can choose our path in life. We can influence a certain amount of events that affect us. Consequently, we are initiators and creators as well as being in the stream of history.

Each individual person is concerned primarily with him/herself. I must endeavour to fashion the world to suit me. No matter how scientists, journalists, teachers or newscasters try to focus my attention on the material world I will relate what they say or teach to me. I will dominate my world. If I go on holidays to China, Greece, Egypt or Australia I will relate my new experiences to what I already know. On my return I may have pictures of wonderful sites that I visited, but my actual experiences will be different to any other person's experiences. No other person can sense, observe and memorize exactly as I can but more importantly no other person interprets feelings and ponders on perceptions and sensations in the same way as I do. Every person possesses this existential privilege, an existential privilege that can leave each individual with moments of uncertainty, fear and loneliness.

When I fall asleep, I sleep alone. My thoughts and my dreams relate to me, I am the central character. No matter how the world tries to impinge on me, control me and condition me, it is me, and me alone, who is aware and makes sense of it all. I take in what I want to take in. I reject or ignore aspects of the outside world that do not appeal to me, or, that I choose to discard. I may do this consciously or unconsciously. Another human being may imprison me and leave me with only walls to look at. It then appears as if that person has restricted my thinking and directed it in a particular way. However, I may accept or refuse to accept what is presented to me. I may refuse to look at the wall and even if I do stare at the wall my thoughts may be on something else. I live in my world.

Perhaps this reasoning could be challenged. I am walking through a field when a thunderstorm begins. The rain pours down. I have no choice but to feel the rain. The rain will impinge on me. Similarly, if I am caught in a fire and my clothes are set ablaze I will feel the heat and the pain. The outside world, in this case the fire, is impinging on me. I am not choosing. The outside world is forcing itself on me. The problem with this argument is that I am taking *my body* to be me. My body feels the rain, or, the heat. My body is composed of a combination of material elements. All the elements of the world fluctuate and interact with each other. Material objects impinge on other material objects.

The mind belongs to a non-material category. It plays a different role to the physical, material body. The mental and physical interact with each other but in a different way to how the physical interacts with the physical. By and large I control and fashion the world to my ends. We must, of course, determine those ends but that is the subject matter for another day. The physical body wears out in time. Scientific research has established that the cells of the body are constantly wearing out and being replaced by new cells. All the cells of the body are renewed within a calendar year. The body that I have today, like the water in a river, will be different tomorrow and totally different this time next year. In that wearing out the body does not disappear. Cells are simply being recycled. They rejoin the elements and compounds of the earth. A different logic pertains to mental processes. The mind is not composed of material elements and compounds. Thoughts do not return to the earth. Thoughts may be transmitted to another mind. They may be materialised in works of art or in our everyday life's undertakings. Many ideas are carried into the next generation. Modern civilisation has evolved as a result of such a transferral of thoughts. Today's world is yesterday's dream and today's dream is tomorrow's world.

Human thinking has created and invented what we use and admire today. Thoughts are passed on through books, works of art, buildings, engineering achievements, medical advances, psychological, educational and other human achievements. Thoughts are not buried or cremated as bodies are. The mind influences and controls the body. Friedrich Hegel an eighteenth century German philosopher believed that human cognition is part of the flow of history. Our thinking changes from generation to generation. No thought is true forever but a thought can be true and correct from a particular perspective and at a particular time in history. *Situation Ethics* aims to put such a philosophy into practice. According to *situation ethics* nothing is intrinsically right or intrinsically wrong. Each act can be judged only in the context of the time and circumstances of the act and the disposition of the person at the time of the performance of that act. Here, human thinking is defined in terms of the flow of history and evolution. This determines our place in the world, how we think and how we act. Right and wrong are judged in an historical context.

Hegel saw human reason as dynamic, as process. We cannot detach a philosopher or a thought from their historical context. The world spirit is progressing with history. History shows how humanity has evolved and progressed towards ever-increasing self-knowledge. According to Hegel history has a purpose. Human history is an expression, a demonstration, an illumination of the evolution of the mind as it advances to ever greater rationality and liberation.

Historicity sees humanity as a changing product of changing conditions. Accordingly, the nature of the person can never be adequately expressed in fixed formulae. Wilhelm Dilthey, one of the chief advocates of historicity, was critical of philosophers who claimed that the mind could grasp physical objects. He was sceptical of the view that subjective elements could enter into experiencing physical objects. For both Hegel and Dilthey the most significant of our experiences are our relations with other humans. Hegel held that outside the historical process there is nothing that can determine truth. History is a chain of reflections.

We may need to inquire into how our culture, religion, views and thoughts have originated and evolved. Our beliefs on issues such as the origin and destiny of the human mind, the existence of God and acceptance of a particular moral code stem from either an Indo-European, or, a Semitic origin. The Indo-European culture had its origin in an area around the Black Sea. From there its influence spread out in all directions. Tribes from that region went north to Scandinavia and Russia, tribes also travelled south and east to India and Israel, while other tribes moved south / west to Greece, Italy and Spain and others went directly west to central Europe, Germany and France. The Indo-Europeans believed in many Gods. This is Polytheism.

The Semitic culture was quite different to that of the Indo-Europeans. This culture originated in Arabia. Semitic culture spread through both Christian and Islamic teachings. The Semitic people believed in one God as do their offspring religions today, Christianity, Muslimism and Judaism. This is Monotheism

Indo-Europeans saw history as cyclical. There is no beginning and no end to history. In the Semitic culture history is linear. God created the world and one day the world will end. Irrespective of our perspective in this regard, history plays a major part in our makeup. We are part of the stream of history. We could quite easily be led to conclude that history controls our lives and destiny, that history and the evolutionary process of nature control everything. We are part of that evolutionary process. We are involved in the making of history too, but history would flow with or without us, just as the natural order does. Historicity may recognise that the mind plays a different role to that of the body, but with regard to individuality, personal choice and free will, it ignores or fuses them into an ever flowing continuous human history.

Perhaps an intelligent being makes and shapes history. My intellect can plan, design and arrange the world to suit my needs and can help to shape the future of the human race. When we speak of having a mind and a body we do not mean a brain and a body. The brain, like the rest of the body, (as it is part of the body) needs material sustenance to remain alive and active. It receives that sustenance through food, water, heat, air and shelter. The mind, being non-material, requires a different type of sustenance.

Philosophy is concerned with human existence and the operation of the mind as well as with the material world. The mind is not to be confused with personality or character that are formed and developed through nurture. Character and personality are influenced by conditioning, indoctrination and education. The mind and the character of the person are categorically different. A person's character and personality are identifiable and observable through his/her behaviour, expression and speech. The mind is creative and unpredictable. It is always active. It cannot be measured.

If we could isolate the mind, see it apart from the body then it would be easier to analyse its operations. When we speak about a person we think mostly about that person's mind. Yet a person is not just a mind. The combination and interaction of both mind and body make up the person. We can comment on the character, personality and will power of a person. We can determine his/her appearance, height, weight and strength. We like to place each individual person in a particular slot. It is easy to do this in terms of physical attributes. But the slot that we want to place a person in pertains particularly to his/her mind. By reaching an understanding of the character, personality and material make-up of a person it might appear that we can then present a definition of that person. That is not the case.

In recent years attempts have been made to understand the person in terms of his/her aura. This aura can be attractive or repulsive as the person wishes it to be, or, it may be attractive to some, repulsive to others. This aura is like a cloud or atmosphere that envelops the person. Within the cloud resides the person who is like the sun radiating light and heat through the atmosphere. All the light will not get through. We may need more than simple observation in order to see, feel and sense the person within that cloud.

Another means of trying to know the person is through an understanding of enneagrams. According to this theory there are nine personality types. Every person possesses one, or, a combination of those types. However, each individual is predominantly one type. Personalities are numbered one to nine and the person is referred to as a **one** or a **three** or an **eight** **etc.,** type personality. According to this theory the **one** type personality is a perfectionist, with anger as a passion and serenity as a virtue. **Two,** is a helper, pride is the passion and humility the virtue. **Three,** is an achiever, the passion is deceit and the virtue is truth. **Four,** is artistic with envy as a passion and equanimity as a virtue. **Five,** is an observer, avarice is the passion and detachment the virtue. **Six,** is a supporter, the passion is fear. This personality type sees courage as the real virtue. **Seven,** is an optimist, with gluttony as a passion and temperance the virtue. **Eight,** is a leader, the passion is lust and simplicity the virtue. **Nine,** is a mediator, laziness is the passion and diligence the virtue. Those who advocate this theory endeavour to get one personality type to take on the best aspects of another type, a complimentary type perhaps.

Some spiritual leaders and preachers encourage people to improve or develop their relationship with others and with God through an understanding of their own personality type in the first instance, followed by an understanding of, and, tolerance for other personality types. Each person must try to adjust his/her own personality to improve the good aspects and shed the aspects that are negative, self destructive or offensive to others. The second step is to accept and realize that there are other personalities in the world. In integrating personality types we develop a better human race, it is alleged. This nurtures and enhances the personality. Self-transcendence and ultimately a relationship with God is the goal.

Transactional analysis is another theory that sets out to explain personality. Transactional analysis sees the individual's personality, not in number types but, as an inter-play of ego states. These ego states are acquired during the person's stages of developments, starting with the infant stage through childhood to adulthood. As we grow and mature from the moment of conception with initial total dependence on parents through childhood and adolescence to adulthood we accumulate a vast amount of knowledge that is stored in the memory. The dependence of the foetus on the mother and the enormous influence of the mother on the foetus in her womb and later as a dependent infant, leave indelible characteristics on the child. They become engraved in the memory.

Childhood is a time of discovery. Joys and sorrows are experienced at a rapid pace during this time, interest is keen and the emotions determine behaviour to a great extent. The child often attempts to assert him / herself, but is subdued and usually forced into submission by authorities. Conditioning plays a part in the person's development and character formation. On reaching adulthood the person is expected to assume responsibility for his/her own actions and behaviour. As the human being advances in life, s/he is expected to take some responsibility for others and for the environment too.

The mature adult has passed through the influences of three distinct types of personality: **the child, the parent**, and **the adult**, all of which go to form a unique personality. These stages and the manner in which a person is affected by them also influence that person's emotional state, behaviour and thinking. An individual who is calm and composed at a particular time may suddenly change and become irrational and even engage in an emotional outburst. This can be explained through an understanding of Transactional Analysis[1] which tries to clarify the interplay between the personalities or ego states (In contemporary psychology sudden changes in behaviour might be explained by the person's position on the autistic spectrum).

Crossed transactions involve a person operating in one ego state and then suddenly reverting to another. Under the influence of the parent-ego state a person may frown, point the index finger, sigh or pat another person on the head. Words like *never, always, should* and *ought* are words often used in this state. Body language from early memories of parent behaviour may also surface in parent-ego state behaviour. Behaviour displayed in this state reflects a nurturing and supportive attitude as well as an authoritative and domineering one. In many family units the mother adopts a nurturing, caring, supportive role while the father displays an authoritative, domineering role.

When the child goes to school the teacher takes on the role of the parent and acts in loco parentis. The teacher may adopt a nurturing or an authoritative role. The teacher who leans too much towards the nurturing side may cause some children to play on his/her generosity. The teacher cannot be a mother to all the children at the same time. Children may see the soft hearted teacher as one of themselves and may try to treat him/her accordingly. The very strict, authoritative teacher may cause anxiety in the weak and timid child. The teacher with the ability to balance a supportive role with an authoritative one should gain the respect of his/her pupils and consequently will be most effective as a teacher.

Manifestations of the child ego state include rolling the eyes, shrugging the shoulders, adopting a drooped posture, casting the eyes downwards and even raising the hand for permission to speak. In this ego state we can differentiate between the natural and the adapted child. A child in the natural state expresses him/herself freely and acts spontaneously. The adapted child avoids confrontation but gets what s/he wants by compliance or even by sulking or whining.

As we might expect, in the adult ego state the person makes judgements and tries to be objective. Here the person tries to make sense of the world. This is the state that usually collapses when a person is under pressure. If that happens then the other two states take over. The child-ego state would appear to be the most valuable in that it is here that our sense of wonder as well as discovery, creativity, spontaneity, enjoyment and fantasy originate. Living in the world damages and erases childhood dreams. We become engrossed in the material world. The mind is then compelled to engage in a clandestine manner.

Most people communicate and interact through a combination of ego-states. In certain circumstances one may use his/her intelligence to adapt ego states to his/her own personal advantage. In general, however, the person has little control over his/her personality. Personality and character are formed and nourished through imitation, conditioning and learned behaviour.

Personality is observable. It may not be possible to measure it accurately, but through tests and observations we can give a broad outline of an individual's personality. We can give a person a character reference. This is a report on how one person sees another in terms of his/her social interactions. It also reports on the person's devotion to duty and assesses how s/he communicates and attends to responsibilities in life and in work.

Can we assess and define the mind in terms of the person's store of experiences? If humanity is to be defined in an historical context then we might have to accept that the human mind develops and progresses with acquired experiences. Susan Greenfield says "my particular definition of mind will be that it is the seething morass of cell circuit that has been configured by personal experiences and is constantly being updated as we live out each moment."[2]

Greenfield suggests that "the mind might well be the personalization of the physical brain, and if the personalization of the brain is driven not so much by genes as by individual experiences, then the concepts of memories, mind and self will be very closely related."[3]

Can we rescue the mind from being identified with the brain, with personality and with the many theories of intelligence that have been postulated down through the centuries? To say that the mind is indefinable or that it is definable only in the context of the whole person maybe a simplistic way of treating the mind or merely a strategy to avoid the difficult task of seeking a definition. The mind is not a combination of the five senses and the brain, nor is it the personality. It is not physical in nature and its activities are not physiological.

The mind can operate with greater efficiency, clarity and creativity when the body, including the brain, is asleep or is in a drowsy or daydreaming state. The mind, in a fully conscious state, is ever watchful over the body and over our surroundings. It can, however, become enraptured in the material world. We can be grounded by the body, thus leaving it difficult for the mind to become liberated from material and earthly entanglements. In sleep the mind is liberated.

People that are steeped in the material world are imprisoned in the body. They are buried, so to speak, before they die. Those who can relax and daydream live in a different world. They live in an intellectual world, a world where the mind is free. This is the world of the imagination, a world of fantasy and creativity. The mind never sleeps. In fact it functions best when conscious awareness is dormant. It contains tremendous power and wisdom. It is possible that the mind is linked to an all-powerful universal mind, for its capability is unfathomable, super natural.

The greater part of my mental life is unconscious. We must endeavour to liberate the mind from material attachments. When the mind becomes engrossed in worldly matters it is then imprisoned by the body. The contemporary practical philosophy that I referred to earlier seeks to get the person to engage actively and thoughtfully in every momentary act. This philosophy asks us to get in touch with nature and our environment and to pay more attention to what we sense. We ought to observe our surroundings with greater attention. We should look and see things, listen and heed the sounds around us. We should consciously become aware of the objects that we feel or touch and take time to deliberately taste the food we eat. We should become conscious of, and identify the odours that impinge on us daily as well as actively using our sense of smell. We must not just allow the senses to simply keep in touch with the outside world. We should use our senses to greater effect and consequently develop better, clearer and more accurate perceptions. This practical philosophy makes our living in the world more meaningful and enjoyable.

It would be beneficial to engage this philosophy periodically but it is too material dependent to adopt it as an everyday living philosophy. It would be even more beneficial, as already suggested, to allow the mind to detach itself from the material world more frequently? The person should let go of the cares and worries of life regularly, and, daydream giving the unconscious mind a chance to plan, create and respond calmly to problems.

Unconscious thinking occurs in the absence of conscious awareness. It operates more efficaciously when conscious awareness is in a dormant state. Plans and creations can be intuitively transported from one mind to another. In this way the plans and designs of an unconscious mind may be put into effect by another person. The committed, focused mind may be capable of directly influencing the physical world. *Inexplicable results can be achieved, too, when the mind focuses, connects and communicates with other minds, creating a universal mental field of energy.*

Sigmund Freud, a medical practitioner, devoted most of his medical working life and his writings to understanding the unconscious mind. He invented psychoanalysis. He maintained that many people suffer illnesses both physical and mental as a result of thoughts and desires being repressed into the unconscious mind by the conscious mind. Experiences that a child thinks will elicit disapproval are often suppressed causing some anxiety and confusion. These repressed thoughts and ideas may surface in the form of an illness at a later stage in life.

The key to Freud's revolutionary theory of psychoanalysis is to be found in his Interpretation of Dreams.[4] He maintained that dreams are generally a form of wish fulfilment. Most dreams are an enactment in fantastic or symbolic form of hidden desires buried in the unconscious mind. Unresolved childhood emotional desires or problems that were repressed into the unconscious mind are often given expression in dreams.

Pre-school teachers and counsellors should be available to parents who find it difficult to cope with a child in his/her early years, particularly during the first five years. These are the most important years for character formation. Language development, self esteem, communication techniques, personality and independence of mind should be fostered at this stage in the child's life. Children need plenty of sleep during these early years. They need to dream pleasant dreams. Reading stories with a moral to children at this age is most valuable.

Freud distinguishes a dream's overt expression from its latent content. The latent content can be uncovered and revealed through psychoanalysis. Freud held that repressed sexual desires were the cause of many problems.

His *Oedipus complex* theory holds that a son has an attraction to his mother and a rivalry and hostility towards his father. Daughters have an attraction to their father, and hostility towards their mother, but their attraction to their father is not as intense as sons have towards their mother. Freud called this attraction of daughters to their father and hostility towards their mother the *Electra complex*. Many contemporary Freudian analysts firmly believe that sexual issues, buried in the unconscious mind, still create problems for many individuals. They also suggest that people who feel uncomfortable about Freud's theory may themselves be victims of such repressed desires.

Freud uses a method called *free association* to draw the latent content from the depths of the unconscious mind to the surface of the conscious mind. Under hypnosis a person recalls a dream then through suggestion and questioning expresses spontaneously the significance of the dream. Although some of the evocations or revelations may seem unimportant, even irrelevant initially, these associations could lead to a significant revelation of the dreamer's innermost thoughts and pre-occupations. When the latent content is not spontaneously evoked, subsequent analysis is necessary in order to reveal that latent repressed content.

Carl Jung, who worked with Freud for more than ten years, was unhappy with Freud's method of interpreting dreams through the *free association* technique. He preferred *direct association*. Jung's method directed the person's thoughts towards, and not away from, the original images in the dream. Jung developed a theory of archetypes that appear in dreams. He believed that nine archetypes dominated dreams: The Wise Man, the Trickster and the Great Mother are perhaps the best known of his archetypes.[5] The *Wise Man* may appear in dreams as a teacher, priest, father, doctor or a master magician. Those people represent male authority, healing or destruction. *The Trickster* may appear as a monkey, a fox, a clown, a hare or other mischievous and playful creature or image. *The Trickster* represents havoc and the destruction of an ordered and orderly society.

Jung sees the mother figure as that which has the greatest influence on our psychological development and he saw it as the key to a person's expectations in life. This is a most ambivalent archetype. In some cases it is virginal, heavenly and supernatural as experienced in Christianity. In other cases it is life producing and earthy as in the polytheistic religions. Like the *Wise Man* she has the power to create and to destroy.

The mother figure has an enormous influence on one's personality according to Jung. He maintains that we all expect someone or something to nurture and comfort us in times of stress. Jung believes that psychotherapy may be required in many cases in order to remedy the behaviour patterns exhibited by the person whose mother has not fulfilled the archetypical mother role for the child. Jung outlined and described the huge diversity and variety of personality types that exist. His invention of the terms *introvert* and *extrovert* describe his two most basic types.

For Jung the collective unconscious is the mainspring and source of human psychological life. Jungians today speak of *psychic wholeness* as the objective of Jungian psychotherapy and dream analysis. Jung, like Freud, spent his whole life trying to understand the mind and the thinking process. Through his research and experimentation he concluded that the unconscious mind directs our lives. We may erroneously think that fate determines the vicissitudes of our daily living and our destiny. It is the mind. Conscious awareness is not a more advanced state than unconscious thinking. It is merely a different state.

The attempt to measure intelligence is indicative of our ignorance of an understanding of the mind. It is also indicative of our desire to reduce the mind to a quantitative substance. The mind does not have a quantitative dimension. It falls under the category of potency. We cannot measure potency. We may try to limit or measure the scope of potency, but potency itself is not quantifiable. It does not exist in substantial form. It may remain dormant, awaiting actualisation, but when potency is actualised it is then no longer potency.

The mind emits communicative signals that can be received by other minds. These emissions are similar to radio signals. They can be transmitted and received by another mind, even if that mind is at a very far distance. Telepathy may be explained through this process. In everyday life the mind communicates with other minds through language and through intuition. Intense concentration or mental agitation may cause inexplicable physical disturbances.

Witchcraft and spiritual healers endeavour to tune into other minds without physical interference. The intensely focused, motivated and concentrated mind is capable of achieving inexplicable results. Contemplatives and those who engage in transcendental meditation can exercise incredible power over the physical world. Hypnosis involves one mind getting another person's conscious mind to relax or sleep. In that relaxed state the hypnotist makes suggestions to the other's unconscious mind. Those suggestions elicit a response, often times a response that that person would not make if in a conscious state. That response comes from the incredible store of experiences and information that is hidden or buried in the unconscious mind.

Every person has an extrasensory transmission faculty and extrasensory perception. A person's extrasensory faculty can emit mental signals or vibes that can be perceived by another person's extrasensory faculties. What we call the sixth sense is very different to what we know about the five senses that we are familiar with. This so-called sixth sense is not a sense in the material sense of the word. The five senses are feelers that come in contact with the material world. They absorb what they sense and convey their findings to the brain for analysis and perhaps a reaction or response. The sixth sense is a mental power that is capable of tuning into another person's mental life. We call it extra sensory as it is not dependent on the senses for transmission or reception. It is outside the domain of the bodily senses. It is in the category of the supernatural.

The type of personality one possesses is determined mostly as a result of nurture. Personality is an amalgamation of overt behavioural mannerisms, habits and characteristics particular to an individual person. It includes the social and personal traits that an individual projects through language. We can explain personality as the observable and identifiable characteristics portrayed by a person and how those characteristics relate to, and compare with other people.

The mind is the driving force of the person. It is as a result of this driving force that the person communicates and achieves success as a human being. Achievements beyond the animal state are attained as a result of the person's intellectual capacity. Planning, analysing, inventing, designing and creating are intellectual traits. While these abilities may have their origin in the prefrontal cortex of the brain they are non-material in essence.

The human being possesses an instinctive desire to survive just like all animals on earth. Mental processing is not instinct at an advanced level.

Instinct is predominantly a survival trait. It is easy to confuse both. The human being can soar far above the survival stage. S/he can refuse to live in the animal world. S/he can offer his/her life for some particular cause. Visionaries, artists, poets, philosophers rarely achieve results in order to gain material or monetary rewards, for worldly possession or for survival purposes. Through mental processing they actualise or make concrete a thought or an idea.

Rationalism places undue emphasis on the mind by excluding the material aspect of the person while materialism emphasises the material aspect at the expense of the mind. We have both a mental and physical dimension. The mental dimension includes ideas, abstract concepts, thinking and dreams. These are not material in essence and are beyond the reach of the senses. Physical phenomena are observable, audible or sensible in some way by means of one or a combination of the five senses. They are empirically verifiable. We cannot have a scientific approach alone to an understanding of the person.

There is an anti-mentalist tendency pervading contemporary thinking. This anti-mentalist notion emanates from the assumption that, unless we can eliminate mental phenomena, we will have to contend with a whole plethora of phenomena that exist outside the realm of science. However, there is also a tendency pervading a great deal of philosophical thinking that sees all knowledge in subjective terms. Those philosophers maintain that objective knowledge does not exist.

It is true that each and every person has a different view of the world. It is also true that there is no epistemologically objective view of the world. But that does not mean that there is not an objective world. Each person's having a different view of the world, does not mean that we all live in objectively different worlds. That conclusion is known as the *epistemic fallacy*. "The mistake involved in the epistemic fallacy is the failure to distinguish epistemological objectivity from ontological objectivity. Even if we know the world only in epistemically partisan ways, it hardly follows that there is no ontologically objective world there to be known."[6]

In our contemporary world the notion of a spirit or mind lodging within the body is mocked and ridiculed. It is the manner in which language is used that causes the confusion. According to Gilbert Ryle, this official doctrine (of separation) hails chiefly from Descartes. A person's body and mind are linked together, *but after the death of the body the mind may continue to exist and function.* Ryle sarcastically refers to this official doctrine as ***the dogma of the Ghost in the Machine.*** [7] He sees the person as a unit, one undivided being. Mental processes cannot operate independently of the body, he maintains. He may be correct in this. But on the other hand the unconscious mind may be capable of functioning without the involvement of the body.

As we have noted, many of today's scientists venerate the human brain. "Neuroscientists themselves often refer to the brain as though it was an autonomous little man lurking beyond the neurons."[8] There is undoubtedly contact between the mind and the brain but to say they cannot function independently of each other has never been proven. The assumption that the mind does not exist independently of the brain is unverifiable. Science itself is uncomfortable with unverifiable assumptions.

Any attempt to empirically prove or disprove the existence of non-material being is unrealistic and unachievable. We cannot apply verification methods, pertinent to the physical world, in order to prove the existence or non-existence of non-material mental or spiritual phenomena. There is no valid reason why we should accept empirical observations as true and at the same time refuse to accept that conceptual observations can be true. We rely on deductive reasoning in order to test deductive reasoning. We rely on memory in order to evaluate, clarify and verify memory claims.

Gilbert Ryle maintained that the logic of our everyday use of language is very confusing and that our thinking and our language may be at variance with reality.

The mind "is not the name of another person, working or frolicking behind an impenetrable screen: it is not the name of another place where work is done or games are played."[9] Ryle hoped that language analysis would eliminate this misunderstanding and show a person to be a single biological unit. Wittgenstein and Ryle emphasised the absurdity of using language specific to one category in order to analyse, explain or even talk about issues pertaining to another category. Ryle calls this *the category mistake.*"[10] We cannot apply criteria pertinent to one category to matters relating to another category. Wittgenstein makes the same point, but with even greater emphasis and at greater length. Wittgenstein says that we cannot apply the rules of one game to adjudicate on issues pertaining to a different game. Each game has its own set of rules. Language is the same;

we have *language games,* we cannot apply the rules of one language game to another language game.

Descartes' giving priority to the mind over the body has been ridiculed by many philosophers. Bruce Hood says that most adults may know the scientific position that the mind is a product of the brain and that it depends on the brain but "are likely to still make the same mistake as Descartes in thinking that the immaterial mind acts directly on the material brain"[11] We do not have evidence to support the claim that the material world is superior to the mental, or, that the material world is the only world. The modern person aligns him/herself with Empirical Science for three reasons mainly. (1) We live in the material world, we sense it; see, feel, hear, taste, and smell it and consequently accept it as the only world. (2) We are too apathetic, too busy and too scientifically orientated to inquire into a mental or spiritual world. (3) We have seen so many myths crumble down through the centuries, and particularly in the most recent twentieth century, that we do not wish to give allegiance to anything that is not empirically verifiable. We fear that we may face possible embarrassment at a later stage if we believe in something that is not sensible or scientifically provable.

If we believe that a spiritual world does not exist because we have no experience of it then we are basing its non-existence on our experience. The twentieth century witnessed the emergence of a philosophy called Positivism. This philosophy set about establishing a theory of truth known as The *Verification Theory* of meaning. This theory held that propositions, theories and beliefs that cannot be empirically verified are meaningless. The criterion for establishing the truth of propositions and theories was through empirical verification. By its own criterion this verification theory itself is meaningless.

Karl Popper, a philosopher of the same period came up with another theory. He introduced a new criterion of truth; he called this the *Falsification Theory.* [12] According to Popper we must not depend on verification alone to establish truth, we must also look to falsification. If something is not verifiable then we ought to query if it is falsifiable. Seeking empirical verification for the reality of the mind is impossible since the mind is non-material. We cannot empirically verify the existence of the mind, the thinking process, or, an idea. Neither can we falsify their existence. How do we know that they exist then? *The mistake in pursuing this line of argument is that we are taking non-material being to be objectively verifiable or falsifiable. Language analysis shows the folly of such reasoning.* We cannot apply the same language game rules to animate and inanimate beings. Thinking and physical activity belong to two totally different language games. Mind and matter are categorically different.

The mind may be capable of inquiring into the existence of non-material being, the mind itself being non-material in nature. For this reason, we must give Descartes credit for setting out to establish the existence of the thinking mind by means of the thinking mind. Having established the existence of the mind through language or the thinking process we hardly need to continue to seek empirical, observable and scientifically verifiable proof for its existence. Spiritual phenomena are categorically different to physical phenomena. Laser-beams, x-rays or scanning devices of any sort cannot be used to examine the mind of the person. One mind can influence another and it can persuade that mind to think in a certain way. Responsive thinking is dependent on sensations received from the outside world. Creative thinking is not solely dependent on the material world.

Descartes used the mind to inquire into the mind, that elusive dimension of our being. He engaged in original and reflective thinking. I think, and then I think about that thinking. We are all aware of our own thinking. We do not know what the other person is thinking but we can assume with reasonable justification that s/he is thinking. I know that I am thinking. I can reflect on my thinking. The realisation and awareness of my own thinking does not tell me if another can do likewise. However, just as the senses help to acquire knowledge for us, that knowledge when it is acquired, takes on a non-material dimension. I know that my thinking and ideas can be actualised. Speech, written records and works of art are an actualisation of thoughts. An understanding and acceptance of the fact that my ideas can be realised in material form and verified in writings, works of art, building constructions etc. leads me to believe that other similar tangible works that are not mine are the result of another person's intelligence.

Isn't it reasonable to suggest that we are aware of the material world and can prove its existence only through the mind, the intellectual dimension of our being? Without the ability to create and use measurements and instruments for measuring we could not prove the existence of anything.

We can sense the world of physical being but may not be able to make sense of that sensing without the intellect.

Language, as the embodiment of thoughts is indicative of the other person's having thoughts, which is a consequence of that person's ability to think in order to formulate those thoughts. I articulate my thoughts as I speak. I deduce from this that the other person does likewise when s/he speaks. I can be aware of another person's thinking, just as I can be aware of my own. This is not just intuition or abstraction. It can even be objectively verified through recordings such as art and written works. While the mind is neither tangible nor observable, the results of thinking and intellectual processing are evident and verifiable. The man-made constructed world in which we live with its civilisation, communication networks and techniques, space travel, micro-surgical developments and the computer are manifestations of man's ingenuity, of his/her intellectual ability. This is observable, tangible verification of the product of intellectual processing and human communication. We are using language to reflect on the products of thinking.

Establishing what intelligence is capable of achieving or knowing has encountered even more obstacles than the acceptance of the existence of the mind itself. Epistemology is the branch of philosophy that deals with knowledge. We must be able to state what knowledge is, and, to establish a basis for truth. Epistemic relativism challenges objective truth. According to this theory all our knowledge, values and judgements are socially and historically based. Epistemic relativism holds that our beliefs, values and judgements depend on our circumstances, on the information we have at a particular time, where we stand on the globe and our stage of development in evolutionary terms. Situation Ethics, as we have seen, tried to establish the criteria for morality in the same way, i.e. in relative terms.

If we do not believe in an objective reality we will live in a world of uncertainty. We may not be able to grasp fully the objective world. Our knowledge about the world is subjective. This does not mean, however, that objective reality does not exist. "Epistemologically, all judgements remain provisional, subject to new information or re-evaluation. But we can arrive at what is pretty universally accepted as true – this is elethia, or elethic truth – the truth of reality as such."[13] From the pragmatist's perspective, as articulated by William James, the value of truth depends exclusively on its usefulness.[14]

We need to inquire into how our thinking operates. What makes one person appear brighter than another? Is it possible to teach a person to think? In answering these questions we may need, in the first instance, to take a look at what forms our thinking, characterizes us, and develops our personality. Conditioning, indoctrination and education play a major part in character formation. They play a central role too, in our everyday thinking and responding as well as for how we act, react and behave.

ENDNOTES:

CHAPTER III

[1] Berne, E **GAMES PEOPLE PLAY;** The psychology of human relationships First published by Grove Press N.Y. 1964 Penguin edition London 1968

[2] Greenfield, Susan **THE PRIVATE LIFE OF THE BRAIN** First published in the U.S.A. and Canada by John Wiley & Sons, Inc. 2000 Published in Penguin Books 2001, Reissued 2002 p.13

[3] Ibid. p.14

[4] Freud, Sigmund **THE INTREPRETATION OF DREAMS**. Trans by James Stachey. publ. 1991

[5] Jung's nine archetypes were: the wise man, the trickster, the shadow, the divine child, the anima, the animus, the hero, the persona and the great mother.

[6] M.S. Archer, A Collier and D.V. Parpora - **TRANSCENDENCE** First published by Routledge 2004, p.2

[7] Ryle, Gilbert - *Descartes' myth* in **DESCARTES** – *A collection of essays* Edited by W. Doney. First published in the U.S.A. 1967 – Reprinted by MacMillan & Co. Ltd. London 1970 p.343

[8] Greenfield, Susan **THE PRIVATE LIFE OF THE BRAIN** op. cit., p.30

[9] Ryle, Gilbert **THE CONCEPT OF MIND** op. cit., p.5

[10] Ryle, Gilbert *CATEGORIES (1938)* reprinted in **LOGIC AND LANGUAGE** – Essays by G. Ryle - 2nd series. Edited by Anthony Flew. Published by Blackwell; Oxford. 1951

[11] Hood, Bruce, op. cit., p.143

[12] Popper, Karl **CONJECTURES AND REFUTATIONS**, The growth of scientific knowledge, 4th edition 1972

[13] Archer, M. S. Collier, A. and Parpora, D.V. **TRANSCENDENCE** op. cit., p2

[14] James, William **THE PRINCIPLES OF MATHEMATICS** Vol.1Published by Dover Publications 1950

THINKING
Conditioning, indoctrination and education

At the outset we must distinguish between evolution in the material, physical world and the evolution of the mind. Zeno, who preceded the three renowned Greek philosophers Socrates, Plato and Aristotle, introduced logic as a means of proving or disproving arguments. Through the method of **reductio ad absurdum**, an argument could be shown to be false if it led to a contradiction.

Wonder and awe inspired Socrates to inquire into all aspects of life, animate and inanimate. He pondered on the enormity of the cosmos and the origin of all that exists. Plato, succeeding Socrates, prioritized ideas. He maintained that only that which is unchanging and eternal is real. Material being is ever changing and transitory. His theory of forms aimed to demonstrate how we can reach out beyond the material world and live in a world of ideas. There are many cats, dogs and fish of various sizes, colours and shapes in the world, but they are all formed in the image of one universal ideal cat, dog or fish. He believed that there were ideal forms of universal or abstract concepts, too, such as beauty, truth, and justice as well as mathematical concepts like number and class.

Aristotle played a major role in the evolution of philosophy and the development of logic. He saw philosophy as the discipline of critical reflection. Aristotle held the view that everything has a natural function and strives to fulfil that function. The concept of function, according to Aristotle, could explain the behaviour of everything in the universe. He also applied this principle to Ethics maintaining that the natural function of the human being is to reason, and those who reason best are those who reason in accordance with virtue.

Reasoning discerns the similarity or dissimilarity between two or more concepts. Reasoning operates in two forms, through induction and deduction. Inductive reasoning is reasoning that draws from a number of particular premises or judgements a more general conclusion or judgement. In the deductive process a general principle or rule is applied to a particular case. With practice we can improve our inductive and deductive reasoning. Mathematics and logic are two fields of study that solve problems through those reasoning methods. Litigation procedures use both inductive and deductive methods. For everyday problems, however, it is difficult and unnecessary to apply these rules. Daily encounters are not composed of sets of rules or regular and predictable patterns.

A great number of contemporary educationalists believe that thinking can be taught. Edward de Bono maintains that experience and research are beginning to bear this out. The term *lateral thinking* coined by Cherry Thomas was adopted by de Bono in his attempt to break thinking out of its linear patterns. He wished to see thinking as something that sets out to explore and to develop new perceptions instead of just working harder with existing perceptions. In this sense lateral thinking is closely connected with perceptual thinking. Edward de Bono believed that we can teach perception and wisdom. "Wisdom depends heavily on perception. It is a matter of teaching perception - not just logic."[1]

In the past twenty years attempts have been made in many countries throughout the world to introduce a subject called *Critical Thinking* into schools' curricula. The major difficulties encountered in those attempts have been with determining the content and range of such a subject domain. Neither a clear unanimous methodology for teaching thinking nor specific subject content for such a domain has yet been established. This leads one to suspect that a subject domain entitled *Critical Thinking* may not be achievable.

Matthew Lipman, in a paper called **Critical Thinking: *what can it be?,*** says that ; "if we consult current definitions of critical thinking we cannot help being struck by the fact that the authors stress the outcomes of such thinking, but generally fail to note its essential characteristic."[2] In another paper, **Misconceptions in Teaching for Critical Thinking,** Lipman having outlined a number of reasons for misconceptions about critical thinking then concludes by saying: *"the failure of efforts to make education relevant during the past two decades stemmed from the peculiar notion that there merely had to be relevant content without any effort to develop relevant skills"*[3] Edward de Bono believes that thinking is a skill and it can and should be taught in schools: "there is need to develop the skill of thinking." He defines thinking as: "the operating skill with which intelligence acts upon experience"[4]

On the other hand, the notion of teaching thinking has been vociferously rejected by John McPeck, a Canadian educationist. He maintains that thinking is not a skill and it cannot be taught. Thinking does not denote any particular skill, or indeed any particular kind of skill. We need knowledge for critical thinking not skills. In the case of "a discussion or argument about some public issue - - - - who is usually able to make the more useful contribution? Is it the person who possesses the relevant knowledge and information or is it the person who has been trained in certain specific skills?"[5] The larger our store of knowledge the greater the volume of data we have to think about. Analytical thinking ought to be included in all areas of teaching and learning. It is an essential element in intellectual processing, but is not the sole constituent of intelligence.

When a person, or any living creature, changes its behaviour as a result of experiences acquired, knowledge gained or something learned, that person or creature is displaying intelligence. A further revelation of intelligence is demonstrated when a person or creature creates or devises an idea or plan and then proceeds to put that idea or plan into effect. For knowledge of material reality to be acquired there must be contact between the senses and the material world.

Polarised views on the question of how knowledge of the external world is acquired should no longer exist. Through experimental research and observations it is now accepted that the prefrontal cortex can operate independently of the senses. This area of the brain may trigger the senses into action and cause them to reach out and absorb the outside world. There are times, too, of course, when the material world causes the person to act, react or respond to events and statements.

The most common everyday conscious thinking process starts with sense experience. That thinking process may be initiated by the prefrontal cortex, or, it may be ignited by the outside material world impinging on the senses. A person may initiate a sense experience in the hope to proceed through a thinking process to gain knowledge but may fail to attain that goal. That person may not get beyond the initial sense experience. The person who initiates a sense experience but does not proceed with it through the process of thinking will have experienced only a sensation; however, some people may proceed through an unconscious thinking process to produce a masterpiece. Many original ideas and creations are conceived and generated in this way.

In general, it is through the conscious thinking process that knowledge of the world is obtained. At this point we will distinguish between *a priori thinking* (creative thinking) and *a posteriori thinking* (responsive thinking). Original thinking and inspirations are manifestations of a *priori* thinking. *A posteriori* thinking involves thinking about acquired knowledge, beliefs or ideas. A priori thinking is deductive, i.e. reasoning from cause to effect. A posterior thinking is inductive, reasoning from effect to cause. Creative thinking can be involuntary too. This is unconscious thinking. We engage in involuntary thinking when we are asleep and when we day dream. Involuntary thinking is often creative. It operates through the imagination and not through direct contact with the sensible, material world.

Since most of our thinking begins with sense experience it is essential, in the school setting, for the teacher to present factual information clearly and to explain and clarify the concepts absorbed or acquired through the senses. It is of paramount importance too, for teachers to clarify generalizations in simple and unambiguous language.

Edward de Bono differentiates between pro-active and reactive thinking. If we equate thinking with language then language for communication purposes can be taken as active, not active in the physical sense, but in the sense that it is constantly changing and it instigates change. One could also speak of creative thinking as active thinking. The contemporary buzz word for creative thinking is proactive thinking. The word active pertains to the physical world. Creative thinking is original thinking. The term create relates to mental conceptions. Activity relates to physical operations. Reactive thinking might be better termed *responsive thinking*. We respond to ideas and to actions that result from other people's thinking processes. Sometimes the response is given almost instantly. An instantaneous response is akin to a reaction, it may undoubtedly have an emotional dimension, but it is responsive thinking. The response may be hasty and given without sufficient deliberation but it is a response nevertheless.

We react to events and ideas too, but that is in the physical domain. Reactions are of the nature of all living creatures. Responses come from an intellect. We may regret a response given instantaneously. That response may have produced a physical reaction. In such cases the physical has overpowered the mental. Our thinking and the thinking of others lead to, and cause actions. Thinking per se, however, belongs to a different category to action.

As we noted in an earlier chapter the mind (the unconscious mind) performs best when the brain and the physical body are in a dormant state. We are constantly thinking. We think while in an unconscious state. We think while we work, play, eat, talk and read. Thinking is progressive and continuous. I cannot take a break from thinking. The brain needs regular rest periods. The mind does not need to rest. Our ability to let go of the material world and allow the mind to think freely and without interruption is perhaps the principal element of intelligence. The more intelligent members of the population make the best use of the unconscious thinking mind to plan and create.

Responsive thinking is dependent on knowledge and experience. If we are called upon to respond to a situation with which we've had no previous experience or knowledge we may need creative thinking. Creative thinking generally involves the mind planning, inventing, composing or creating some idea that is subsequently actualised in oral, written, visual or some other concrete form. Responsive thinking has an instinctual characteristic, perhaps even a survival aspect. It is akin to reflexive action in the physical world.

The eye reacts instantly to some object coming towards it. The touch sense reacts reflexively and instantly to the touch of an extremely hot or an extremely cold object. We will spit out something instantly that we find totally unpalatable, something very bitter. We shrink away from a very loud or shrill sound or from an obnoxious odour. We react, too, to a positive sensation, to a beautiful sight, a pleasant touch, a palatable taste, an attractive scent or harmonious sound. A person may react reflexively to a sense experience. A person who deliberately and consciously repeats that reaction to a subsequent similar sense experience is probably engaging in responsive thinking.

Creative thinking is a higher form of thinking. It is this aspect of thinking that distinguishes humans from all other animals. Creative thinking constitutes the basic and essential ingredient of intelligence. It is difficult, if not impossible, to assess a person's ability to think creatively. It is this creative or original thinking ability that has produced so many great human theories and inventions such as the theory of relativity and inventions like electricity, solar power, air and spacecraft, submarines, computers and motor vehicles. Humankind has also developed ingenious communication techniques: facsimiles, e-mails, the internet, cellular phones and satellite television. Engineering innovations, travelling methods and medical advances that include keyhole surgery, lazar treatment, x-rays as well as oral and intravenous medicines that can help or cure diseases hitherto incurable are all the result of creative thinking. In our everyday use of language we are involved in both creative and responsive thinking. Almost every sentence we use is original in wording and phraseology. However, much of the language we use and the communication we engage in, involves responses to other people's language, ideas and activities.

Dreaming, even day-dreaming, is thinking. This involves the mind operating independently of the body. The body is the physical dimension of the human being. The body has a great deal in common with that of other animals on the planet. It is the mind that distinguishes us as humans. When a person reacts irrationally to a situation the comment is often made that *s/he is only human*. That should be that *s/he is reacting as any animal would*. Being human is a superior state to being animal. The creative and inventive capability of the human mind and its ability to acquire copious amounts of information is beyond comprehension.

For those who are involved in education it is crucially important to keep abreast of new discoveries pertaining to the operations of the human brain. We have already noted the importance of the prefrontal cortex. Both left and right frontal lobes receive and decipher language and other non verbal sounds too. We have noted the importance of Wernicke's and Broca's areas of the brain in speech articulation and language comprehension. It is vital for teachers to pay attention to methods of presenting material and to the appropriate time for its presentation. A crucial ingredient in teaching and learning is accuracy and clarity in concept formation. What, why, and how we memorise and what, why, and how we recall are vitally important questions. It is from an understanding of the operation of memory and through expressive language that we can explain most clearly the thinking process. We must guard against over-verbalised learning, for if the language is not understood, learning will not take place.

Learning is most effective when the language of the lesson is clear, simple, unambiguous and based on knowledge already acquired. If information is presented in isolation from information already in the memory, and, in language that is difficult to comprehend, it will result in the student switching off and subsequently entering a dream world. While the teacher is explaining the decomposition method of subtraction to a class of eight year old children or the theory of relativity to seventeen year olds, some of those students may be in Lapland or Disneyland or swimming in the Mediterranean. The language, the method used and the relevancy of the subject matter at the time of teaching will determine the success or otherwise of the lesson taught.

Reflection involves a connection with the past. We may need to make the past relevant to future action. This process is conducted through language. Reflecting on the past helps us to understand the present. Observing and analysing information including abstract concepts and metaphysical propositions help us to obtain a broader perspective on life and to reach out beyond the tangible to ponder other worlds.

Intelligence includes the mental ability to plan, to execute plans and to respond rationally to ideas and events. As we have seen intellectual processing has a creative and a responsive dimension. Creative thinking involves conceiving ideas and formulating plans and then actualising the ideas and realizing the plans. The intellect, therefore, creates, composes, devises ideas and plans. It is responsible, too, for putting those plans, ideas, compositions and creations into effect. The responsive aspect of intelligence involves responding rationally to other people's ideas and to stimuli outside oneself.

If intelligence involves conceiving ideas and plans and in the actualising of ideas and plans then perhaps we can conclude that the most intelligent people will produce the best ideas and plans and will subsequently actualise their ideas and plans with greatest effectiveness, if allowed to do so unimpeded.

Our thinking influences our beliefs. How we behave is generally a consequence of how we think at a particular time and of how we react to external stimuli. Knowledge acquired through the senses and retained in the memory sustains our everyday thinking. A person may be conditioned to behave in a particular manner. Indoctrination may compel a person to believe in a particular creed or doctrine without explanation or analysis. Education involves teaching people to analyse knowledge and to act with purpose. Education should also encourage the periodic shutting out of the physical world in order to allow the unconscious mind to create and dream.

Before we get to the question of education we will take a closer look at *conditioning* and *indoctrination* and how they may affect our thinking. Conditioning pertains to behaviour. One is conditioned to behave in a certain way. A person can be conditioned to do something. Conditioning may be required when teaching methods are not possible. Infants and young children need to be trained to behave in a certain manner, how to go to the toilet, to wash their hands, hair and teeth. Conditioning is required in order to train young children during their first years at school, too. Teenagers and adults with certain types of brain damage who have suffered from strokes and other physical or mental conditions may need to be trained, retrained or conditioned to behave in a socially acceptable way.

Indoctrination involves beliefs. Indoctrination is not concerned with developing or passing on skills or ways of behaving. A person is indoctrinated when s/he harbours a belief without having any reason for the belief. Indoctrination takes place when beliefs are forced on a person, when a person accepts a doctrine without applying his/her reason or will to it. The indoctrinator may have some moral or psychological power over the recipient, sometimes causing the will to become subdued, submissive or totally dormant. Consequently, the indoctrinated person thinks that he has reason for his beliefs and that his beliefs have been freely accepted by him. Indoctrination occurs when a person deliberately implants an unfounded belief in another without allowing that person an opportunity to use his/her reason to establish or disestablish a foundation for that belief.

If beliefs are forced on a person and that individual subsequently accepts them in such a way that those beliefs are not open to rational evaluation; that is indoctrination. A person may become restricted by his/her beliefs. Such a person does not see the necessity to review his/her beliefs and resulting actions in the light of appropriate information and fresh evidence. If I become indoctrinated in this way my future life is limited. *I am - -*

> *"Trapped in a set of beliefs I can neither escape nor even question;*
> *This is how my options, and my autonomy, have been limited. I*
> *have been shackled, and denied the right to determine, insofar as*
> *I am able, my own future".*[6]

A great deal of our beliefs and opinions are formed by the religious and commonly accepted practices into which we are born. Many people's views are formed without the aid of reasoned analysis but are emotional reflections on the beliefs of their society. Children are expected to hold certain beliefs. This is how society develops and operates. In certain circumstances and for some people this may restrict their freedom. It may adversely affect children's thinking and subsequently enslave them as adults. This is damaging because many children will not be able to question those beliefs or have the reasoning ability to analyse, or raise doubts about them later in life. For this reason they will not be able to apply new knowledge to beliefs that they were forced to accept from earlier years. One of the objectives of education must be to get students to establish reasons for their beliefs. The aim is, not to jettison accepted beliefs and customs, dilute cultural activities or abandon traditions, though some of that may also be necessary, but, to establish a rationale for accepting and retaining beliefs, customs and traditions.

The indoctrinated person holds beliefs that are often irrational. The one who is conditioned performs actions without recourse to reason. The educated person holds beliefs and is conditioned in certain ways of behaving but s/he is aware of this and accepts them as the result of reasoned analysis. An educated person is capable of forming clear judgements deduced from premises that are based on evidence, or, on assumptions that have a logically reasoned basis. An educated person understands the necessity to justify beliefs. That person believes something because there is good reason to believe it.

The question that educators must address is; when, how, and under what circumstances, is a teacher said to be indoctrinating and not educating students? We must emphasise, at this point, that education and indoctrination are not opposing concepts. Indoctrination simply belongs to a different category, the category of beliefs. Education is concerned with the acquisition, analysis, retention and utilisation of knowledge. Education includes reasoning and analysing information as well as forming judgements on the basis of experience.

Education involves more than instruction. It includes learning the cultural and spiritual values of the race. This is recognised by both traditional and progressive education. The school cannot exist simply to "minister to the child's intellectual needs, leaving his moral, social and economic life to his home and his church. The school must be interested in everything about the child."[7] A prime objective of education is for the learner to realize his/ her own potentialities; another objective is that the teacher should help transmit the cultural and spiritual inheritance to the next generation. Music and art are essentially spiritual.

Each child has a right to inherit the cultural and spiritual heritage developed by his/her ancestors. A person has a right to scientific, literary, aesthetic and cultural inheritance and to religious inheritance too. All of these disciplines help to make the individual a more balanced and cultivated person. If a person, in virtue of being human, is entitled to such inheritance, then that person is entitled to an objective analysis of that inheritance too. This entitlement must be offered through a medium that is unbiased. That medium maybe a person who possesses a passion and enthusiasm for his subject-matter, who will transmit sincerity, conviction and honesty, but who will also expose presented material to objective analysis, in so far as that is possible and appropriate.

We need to examine the factors that characterise us and influence our thinking. Life's experiences have the greatest bearing on our thinking. Character is displayed by actions. Our thinking determines most of our actions. John Dewey, the renowned American educationist, maintained that being alive involves experiencing. The purpose of education, according to Dewey, is to guide experience in directions that are more beneficial than if left unguided. He did not see experience as categorised into compartments but as something continuous and progressive.

Progressive education, taken to the extreme, does not want to interrupt one's natural experiencing. It aims to facilitate experiencing but not to change, direct, redirect or halt a person's propensities. Misguided experience could be as damaging as indoctrination. Children need guidance in caring, social behaviour, spiritual, moral and ethical development as well as in cultural and religious matters. This is the essence of character formation.

Teachers must inculcate in students a sense of justice, sincerity and truthfulness. They ought to guard against teaching anything that will damage a person's character, well-being and freedom. Refusing to inform someone adequately of something that may have harmful effects his/her life is as serious as telling him/her an untruth leading to similar adverse consequences, both involve and result in misleading another person. When a teacher sees it as necessary to instil a certain belief in students s/he must outline reasons for the belief and establish, where possible, a truth foundation for that belief. In doing this, the teacher ought to search for evidence and endeavour to base the belief on a reasonable foundation. Beliefs should have a personal value for the individual. A person should be able to justify for him/herself the reason for holding a belief.

It is not sufficient to instil or even present beliefs on the basis of their being accepted by the majority of people or because they were accepted by our ancestors. Beliefs ought to have sufficient worthiness for one to be able to say that it makes sense to accept them. Beliefs should be worth inquiring into. Discarding beliefs should create a void that would necessitate investigation. There ought to be, in other words, a sound reason for holding beliefs. They should possess a personal value.

The teacher must not be a medium for passing on prejudices. This could damage a student's ability to reason objectively. The teacher should inculcate a sense of security in the student while passing on traditional values. These values, however, require constant review and analysis. A teacher should not remain totally uncommitted. A teacher who opts out of teaching something is making a decision. Refusing to teach something that may be of value to a child is wrong. Attempting to make the world better according to my standards but within my limited knowledge, experience, and ability is not my role as a teacher.

Teachers must respect children in their care. It is regrettable that many systems of education produced by political regimes under the influence of global capitalism; endeavour to mould children as objects. They want to steer and coral them into a particular way of thinking and behaving. The bulk of what children are taught is of a materialistic nature. They are conditioned or programmed in such a way that they may develop and display the characteristics desired at a particular time. Materialistic gravitation draws society towards conforming to a unified way of thinking. Because of this, many parents are reluctant and unwilling to give direction or advice to their children. They fear that they may not produce the desired and required product. Those parents think that experts ought to be employed in every field. They believe that the school or television will lead and direct their children towards the proper, universal approach to life's problems. They are led to believe that the acceptable object must be produced.

When a person is indoctrinated, that person will follow, conform, react or partake in something without using his/her reason. Such a person is unlikely to initiate, invent, lead or create. In our contemporary world the value of spiritual education in the curriculum is diminished and in many jurisdictions it is discarded. Science is elevated. Spiritual education is seen as speculation while education, pertaining to the material world is justified because the material world is empirically verifiable. Philosophical and theoretical pursuits are viewed as meanderings. They are empirically and scientifically unverifiable and consequently are of little practical value. The propagation of such a notion is deceptive. We are intellectual beings.

The teaching of doctrines without explanation or analysis violates students' rights to be treated as **persons** or **as ends.** People cannot be treated simply as means to ends. If a teacher teaches a doctrine but intends to explain that doctrine as soon as possible afterwards or as soon as the child is capable of understanding it then that teacher can hardly be accused of indoctrination. Knowledge acquisition and the application of that knowledge in order to improve the life of the person spiritually and materially is the goal of education. Education includes the acquisition of information of a spiritual and material nature as well as the learning of social, physical and artistic skills. It also includes the teaching and learning of methods of reasoning, particularly inductive and deductive reasoning and of course information analysis. Acquired knowledge ought to improve one's standard of living and outlook on life. This does not mean the person's material standard of living only but also his/her spiritual well being.

Indoctrination implies the teaching and the acquisition of a doctrine. Many doctrines are worth acquiring. Doctrines that are exposed to scrutiny and analysis are generally worthy of study. Those who refuse to expose a doctrine to analysis may be guilty of indoctrination. Indoctrination occurs when someone is taking advantage of a privileged role to influence someone in his/her care in a way that is likely to leave the influenced person incapable of assessing evidence on its own merit. Indoctrination is seriously harmful if it adversely affects the life of a person.

A teacher who refuses to teach a subject on the curriculum that a child can understand and cope with is indicating that his/her beliefs and opinions are preferable to those in that subject. If we refuse to teach or critically analyse a controversial issue we may be guilty of accepting its validity without question, or, rejecting it without critical analysis. This is unacceptable teaching for it allows children to develop into adults with an uncritical attitude.

For a person to base the non-existence of a spiritual reality on the fact that s/he has never experienced a spiritual reality is to base that non-existence on his/her own experience. Positivism aimed to dispose of metaphysics. In order to achieve this it introduced the verification theory of meaning.[8] Positivists would not even allow discussion on a transcendent reality. For them the notion of *transcendence* is meaningless. Positivists seemed to think that scientific criteria could be applied to a spiritual form of life. Wittgenstein, as we have seen, in his *language –games theory* maintained that the application of criteria pertaining to one form of life to criteria from another form of life is illogical, irrelevant and non-sense.

There are theorists who believe that the main proof of God's existence is to be obtained through religious experience. They maintain that, "religious experience is the primary motivation for religious belief, and, as such, is no more likely to be a total illusion than any other form of experience."[9] Neuroscientists have located an area in the brain that they believe can give intense feelings of spirituality and even a sense of mystical presence. Rita Carter in her book entitled; *Mapping the Mind* refers to a Canadian neuroscientist Michael Persinger of Laurentian University who has claimed to have "even managed to reproduce such feelings in otherwise unreligious people by stimulating this area,"[10] which is situated in the temporal lobe. If this is the case then God may have created in us this capacity to reach out and try to unite with Him. "Nevertheless, it is easy to see that being able to get your God experience from a well-placed electrode could at the very least undermine the precious status such states are accorded by many religions."[11]

It could also be claimed, however, that if the stimulation of an area of the brain can create feelings of spiritual transcendence, then this area could be the centre where the spiritual and temporal meet. Stimulation of this part of the brain may be a method of releasing the earthly connection of the physical to the spiritual. It is as reasonable to acknowledge that this stimulation relaxes the material dimension of the person thereby allowing the spiritual to function uninterrupted, as to suggest that this stimulation creates a spiritual feeling in the physical brain.

When atheists assert the non-existence of God that assertion is based on their own observations and earthly experience. They may have never experienced faith in a spiritual life. Faith can profoundly influence the physical world. The mind can communicate and receive information through intuition as well as through the senses and the brain. We can intuitively perceive something that cannot be explained in physical terms. We may need to have faith in the power of the mind.

Thinking is process. It is progressive and continuous. Like water in a river thinking is never static but constantly changing. *We cannot refuse to think. We are compelled and condemned to think.* The condemnation to think may be most poignant for the young active person on realizing that s/he is inflicted with quadriplegia as a consequence of an accident

A person's ability to think is one of the essential ingredients of human intelligence. Oral, written and body language are the vehicles for communicating thoughts. We can also communicate thoughts and ideas through other media, for example, art in all its forms; including music, fine art, sculpture, architecture etc. Thoughts are actualised or materialised language. As soon as thinking becomes a thought it is no longer potency or process.

The sleeping and the unconscious person may lose awareness of his/her surroundings but will not cease to think. Thoughts are the product of thinking. A thought taken from the process of thinking can be analysed and compared with other thoughts just as a bucket of water taken from a flowing river can be analysed and tested. A thought can be made concrete, sketched, sculptured and produced in many forms including oral and written language.

Thinking ability depends on intelligence. The intellect is not a material substance. It differs categorically from the sense faculties. Thinking includes conceiving, judging and reasoning. The mind can judge and analyse acquired information. The intellect abstracts the essence from objects and beings in the world

Thinking is undertaken by a unique individual in a unique situation and at a period of time that is unique. Like the water in a river this thinking, in this time, place and in these circumstances cannot be repeated. Material substance, such as water, can be analysed. A captured thought can be analysed too, not by scientific instruments but by another mind. This is not only a manifestation of our own existence and thinking but also a manifestation of another person's existence and ability to think.

Psychological assessments, by and large, assess the product of thinking. From the results of an assessment the administrator of the test then goes on to quantify the person's intelligence which includes the depth and range of the thinking process. The product of the thinking does not account for all aspects of thinking. The results of the analysis of a bucket of water taken from a river will not tell us the speed of the flowing water, the depth or breadth of the river or the ingredients contained in the rest of the water in that river. Similarly, the results of an intelligence test will not confirm the ability of the person to create, choose, imagine and respond to novel or unexpected situations and events.

Thoughts that are not actualised remain as shadows. Shadows do not exist as the objects of which they are a reflection exist, but they exist, nevertheless. They have a different type of existence. They do not have substantial form. Heat exists in a different way to that of the source of the heat, the coal, oil, gas etc. What kind of existence does a river have? Can a river exist without the water? We may hear of a 'dried up' river. That could imply that the bed of the river is the river. This is nonsense. The river consists of the water and the river-bed. The water and the river-bed are embedded in the concept 'River'. A tree and the shadow of the tree have a different existence. The shadow is not included in the concept *tree.* The tree can exist without the shadow but the shadow of the tree cannot exist without the tree. A shadow's existence is dependent on an object and on light. The movement of the object or the intensity of the light will distort or may even obliterate the shadow.

The mind does not exist as *the shadow of the tree* exists. The shadow plays no part in the life or the existence of the tree. The mind is an essential aspect of the human being. The mind exists more like the water in the river. The water is constantly moving. Without the water the river would not have a meaningful existence. The water is the lifeblood or soul of the river. We could not swim, row a boat or fish in a river without water. It might have a physical shape and depth, a bank and bridges over it, but it could not be called a river. The water in a river is constantly moving. It feeds and protects fish and other water living creatures. It is the defining aspect of the river. Similarly, the mind is the defining aspect of the person.

The mind is constantly thinking and that thinking is ever changing. The mind plays a major part in directing the body in everyday living and in determining the destiny of the person. The mind plans, analyses, remembers, recalls, imagines and reflects. To speak of the mind as the Ghost in the Machine is to trivialise it. We think of a Ghost as a figment of the imagination, something invisible and unreal, a phantom. We want to show that there is a physical reason for every occurrence, a natural not a supernatural cause.

In what sense does the mind exist? It is not tangible, visible, audible or perceptible as material objects are. Imagination is an essential operating component of the mind. Imagination can take me to Paris, Rome or New York in just an instant. I can see in my mind's eye the CN tower, the Tiber River, the Louvre or the Eifel Tower. I can have a similar thought to a friend, who is in Sydney, at precisely the same time. We have noted the uniqueness of each and every thinking operation, yet the thinking of two people can be almost identical, in process and content, even at a very long distance apart. This is unimportant as far as the thinking is concerned. It merely detaches the thought from time and place. Two people having the same thought at the same time with no apparent reason and with no direct circumstances to trigger the same thought is called telepathy. Others, in amazement may use the phrase 'de ja vou'. The mind is always in an operative mode. During sleep it dreams. In the dreaming state the mind is busy solving problems, reflecting, reviewing, analysing and planning.

It is widely accepted that we use only a small percentage of our brain-power during our life time and in everyday living. So if we could use our brain to its full potential we would achieve so much more in life. *Consequently, if we could make more and better use of the brain we would become more intelligent,* is the implication from that premise. This implies that the brain makes us intelligent. However, if we examine closely the contemporary view of intelligence we see that intelligence is often measured in terms of behaviour and energy output. Increased brain-power will certainly change behaviour and raise energy levels just as a stronger generator will use more power and consequently will produce a greater amount of energy.

When we say that *were we able to use 90% or 100% of our brain we would achieve almost anything* we are making no mistake. But in using the words *were we able,* or, *if I could use 100% of my brain,* I am pronouncing in that utterance that there is an 'I' that can get the brain to function at 90% or 100%. Surely it is not the brain that gets the brain to function at a higher level. I am not using my brain to its full potential. This is no different to saying that in running the race I did not use the muscles of my body to their full potential. If I did, I could have won the race. We are told that motivation resides in a certain area of the brain, but we cannot perform surgery on motivation in order to examine it or improve it.

The mind may fail to direct or focus full attention on the brain or on the senses.

The mind may be attending to, or focusing on more sublime things. One mind may influence another. This can lead to a change in thinking and behaviour in the person being influenced. When the mind uses the imagination, to take a person to Rome, Paris, Los Angeles, The Great Wall of China, South America, Australia or Africa, is that less important than using the brain to operate a computer, to communicate on a mobile phone, or to conduct business for monetary gain? It is impossible for an assessor to measure the imaginative potential of the mind. Engagement in imaginative pursuits is often seen as time wasting, idling and day dreaming. Could a psychologist use those words in an assessment report and still retain credibility?

ENDNOTES:

CHAPTER IV

[1] de Bono, Edward **TEACH YOUR CHILD HOW TO THINK**
Published Viking 1992, Penguin edition 1993 p.8

[2] Lipman, Matthew **CRITICAL THINKING:** *What can it be?*
Institute for Critical Thinking – Resource Publication U.S.A.
Series 1, Vol. 1, 1988 p. 1

[3] Lipman, Matthew **MISCONCEPTIONS IN TEACHING FOR
CRITICAL THINKING** – Institute for Critical Thinking –
Resource Publication Series 2. No.3. 1989 p.8

[4] de Bono, Edward **TEACH YOUR CHILD HOW TO THINK** - op
cit. p. 6 and p.8

[5] McPeck, J. **TEACHING CRITICAL THINKING:** dialogue and
dialectic – Routledge, N.Y. and London 1990 p.4

[6] Siegel, Harvey **EDUCATING REASON, Rationality, Critical
Thinking and Education,** Routledge N.Y. and London 1990 p.88

[7] Rafferty, M. **PROGRESSIVE EDUCATION: The lively corpse.**
A paper by Dr. Rafferty to the 5th Anniversary Conference of
The Reading Reform Foundation. New York 4th August, 1966 –
speaking about J. Dewey p.3

[8] Positivism The Verification theory of truth – see Chapter 3

[9] Archer, M.S. Collier, A. and Parpora, D.V. **TRANSCENDENCE** op.cit.,p.26

[10] Carter, Rita **MAPPING THE MIND.** op. cit., p.13

[11] Ibid. p.14

CHAPTER V

DEFINING INTELLIGENCE
Emotional Intelligence & Multiple Intelligence

There are two perspectives pertaining to the definition of intelligence. On the one hand there are those who maintain that the meaning of intelligence is too broad for definition. The theories of Emotional Intelligence and Multiple Intelligence could be placed in that category. They postulate an open ended definition of human intelligence. On the other hand are those who believe that intelligence is definable and its scope and limits are measurable. Science in general and psychology in particular fall under this category. For those disciplines, intelligence can be explained through an understanding of the physical operations of the brain. We may not have the definitive answer yet, but it is awaiting discovery.

Some of my thoughts and ideas can be materialised. They can be physically and overtly displayed and recorded. I can also witness the fruits of other people's ideas. This is empirical verification of the other's ability to think. Another person's ability to communicate with me in language, through dialogue and writing is a demonstrable manifestation of that person's intellectual existence and thinking ability. When a person touches an object, smells or tastes something and then utters words like, *nice, sweet, sour, bitter* or *noxious* I can identify instantly with the words uttered to express the meaning of the sensation, perception or thought that that person is having and conveying. This conclusion is arrived at from my own previous experience and resulting thoughts. I can conclude from that, that others sense and perceive as I do. They also use language as I do.

When a person utters a word or makes a gesture to express a physical sensation or experience that utterance communicates a thought, an idea or an experience to me and to others. All animals have a similar, albeit, less developed capacity to communicate. Birds chirping as they locate food and animals of prey screeching as they kill their victims are manifestations of this communicative ability. At the human level we communicate mainly through language that can be written or spoken and stored in the memory for later use. We communicate, too, for pleasurable purposes, to gratify the imagination and of course to acquire knowledge. Language is more than a communicative tool for survival purposes. It includes creative thinking. When I put my plans and ideas into effect and produce something that is observable, tangible or audible I know that that is a consequence of my thinking. I can observe the fruits of other people's plans, ideas and creations too. I realise that the fruits of another person's ideas, plans and creations are manifestations of his/her thinking process just as mine are. This is evidence of the other person's ability to think, plan and create. It can tell me that other people can think as I do. However, we have no way of knowing what they are thinking.

Great advances into understanding the brain and its functioning have been made in recent times through research and with the aid of modern technology. We know, through research that the brain-stem, that part of the brain that surrounds the top of the spinal cord regulates breathing and the operation of the body's organs. It plays a part too in controlling reflexes, reactions and general body movements. The brain stem does not think. It regulates and directs the functioning of the body. It controls and ensures survival. In evolutionary terms this was the original brain – the reptilian brain, as we have seen in chapter one.

Scientific discoveries, experimentation and research have revealed that the first animals on earth had a two-layered cortex that surrounded and nestled neatly on top of the brain stem like a ball and socket joint. We are here referring to living creatures that existed between 100 and 300 million years ago. The section of the cortex that circles the brain stem is called the limbic system. It is with this part of the brain that animals and humans filter sensations, make sense of odours, tastes, sights, touches, sounds and then react to those sensations.

The later evolution of the neo-cortex gave the recipient animals additional powers to use their senses more beneficially. The more recent development of the prefrontal cortex gave humans unparalleled reasoning powers. The limbic brain, however, continues to play a crucial role in our defence, survival, communication and gereral behaviour.

In the cortex there exists a pair of almond shaped structures called the amygdala, one on either side. In humans the amygdala is larger than it is in primates, our closest relatives in the animal world. This is the emotional section of the brain. If contact between the amygdala and the rest of the person's brain is severed that person will lack emotional responses to events. S/he will not become emotional or tearful on joyful or sorrowful occasions. Experimental research has shown that the amygdala prompts the body's hormones to react to various stimuli. This enables the person to avoid certain situations and to defend the body against harmful intrusions. It also stimulates the cardio-vascular system, the gut and the muscles.

In a book called *Emotional Intelligence* Daniel Goleman tells us that, in the past, scientists believed that signals entering through our senses were sent to the thalamus, a gland in the cortex of the brain, and, from there they were transmitted to the various areas in the neo-cortex where they were recognised, deciphered and understood. Signals were then sent to the limbic brain from where an appropriate response was delivered. Recent discoveries by neuroscience indicate that a number of neurons connect the thalamus and the amygdala. This connection permits the amygdala to receive sensations directly from the senses. The amygdala immediately sets about a reaction even before the sensation reaches the neo-cortex. This allows the amygdala to produce an emotional reaction before the neo-cortex can give a reasoned response.[1]

Daniel Goleman draws our attention to interesting and valuable discoveries on the workings of the emotional brain: "research has shown that in the first few milliseconds of our perceiving something, we, not only unconsciously comprehend what it is, but, decide whether we like it or not; the 'cognitive unconscious' presents our awareness with not just the identity of what we see, but an opinion about it? Our emotions have a mind of their own, one which can hold views quite independently of our rational mind."[2]

The theory of Emotional Intelligence postulates, not a mind/brain dualism, but, a mind/mind dualism. This theory suggests that we have two minds, an emotional mind and an intellectual mind. However, when we examine the theory more closely we discover that it is not a mind/mind but a brain/brain dualism that is postulated here. The cortex (including the thalamus and the amygdala) is responsible for emotional intelligence. Gut feeling springs from this region of the brain and plays a central role in many people's decisions. Gut-feeling decisions generally pertain to self-preservation and survival. Those decisions are instinctual rather than intellectual. Intellectual reasoning takes place in the neo-cortex area of the human brain. The rational brain takes longer to respond to events. It takes gut-feeling into account but may decide to delay a response to allow time to calculate, consider options and to analyse a situation, statement or event.

Feelings can have a major influence on reasoning. Lack of awareness of feeling can have serious consequences for decision-making. Emotions play an essential role in our setting goals. John Anderson, professor of cognitive psychology and computer science at Carnegie-Mellon University in Pittsburgh, says that emotion has lots of effects on cognition. "One of its roles is to set goals we're trying to achieve."[3]

Some decisions may require gut feeling and experience acquired through the emotions. Formal logic, independent of the emotions and acquired experience will not be able to form satisfactory judgements on some everyday matters such as, interpreting the reasons for other people's decisions. Logical reasoning depends on the truth of a premise in leading to a valid conclusion. Gut feeling and acquired experience may detect an error or falsity in premises. When we need to form a judgement on a person's sincerity, reliability or trustworthiness, formal logic may be insufficient.

The psychologist, Robert Plutchick[4] has produced a list of eight primary and eight secondary emotions. His list of primary emotions are; joy, consent, fear, surprise, sadness, disgust, anger and anticipation. The eight secondary emotions are; optimism, love, aggression, contempt, remorse, disappointment, awe and submission. Each of the secondary emotions is a combination of two primary emotions. Consent plus joy gives love. Fear plus consent gives submission. Disgust with anger produces contempt. Anticipation and joy gives optimism. Anger plus anticipation produces aggression. Sadness with disgust results in remorse. Surprise and sadness gives disappointment. Fear with surprise produces awe.

Through research and experimentation it is now established that the amygdala is the specific area of the brain that deals with emotions. Through the emotions we may be propelled into action. This is an impulsive drive. The word **emotion** comes from the word motion, to move. Impulsive feelings often lead to reactions before the rational brain gets time to consider a response. The amygdala sends instant messages to every major part of the brain. This prepares the body for attack and stimulates areas controlling movements, particularly the cardiovascular system and the muscles.

Can we educate the emotions? Can we prevent impulsivity? Can we stop one from worrying? Chronic worriers seem to be unable to take the advice to stop worrying. By their nature those people persist with worrying when something arises in the mind.

The mind can control the body in resisting impulses. To feel with another is to care. This is empathy. In empathising with a person in pain, sorrow, depression or deprivation we share their distress. This moves people to perform charitable deeds. Putting oneself in another person's place leads one to pursue certain moral principles. People with an 'antisocial personal disorder', sociopaths or psychopaths are unable to empathize with other's pain. "For psychopaths, other people are always an *It*, a mark to be duped, used and discarded."[5]

Many people from various religious persuasions including Christianity, Buddhism, Hinduism, Muslimism, Judaism and even people from a non-religious background have surrendered all their wealth, power and earthly belongings in order to help others. Is it empathy, human survival or religious fervour that motivates those people? It is natural to want to survive and to wish for the survival of the human race. The message preached by all the major religions of the world goes beyond the level of survival. They do not present a moral code based solely on emotional empathy.

Most people empathise with others in times of sorrow and sadness. Psychopaths are an exception. They lack empathy. Research findings indicate that this could be due to an irregularity or damage to their amygdala. It may also be caused by irregularity or damage to connections between the amygdala and the limbic brain, the thalamus, or, the neo-cortex. Research on psychopathic behaviour shows that people with damage to this area have no concerns or worries about punishment that they themselves have to suffer for crimes they commit. This is because psychopaths do not appear to experience fear. Consequently, they do not empathise with the fear or pain of their victims. The immune system, like the brain and the central nervous system, can react to experiences. This reaction can be in the form of a change in behaviour.

Two essential elements of the thinking process are memory and imagination. Memory; retention and recall and particularly our ability to reflect on, retrieve data from the memory bank for spiritual, artistic and pleasure purposes and not simply for survival purposes, sets us apart in the animal world. In order to be able to calculate and communicate at a level above the animal and in order to predict, judge or analyse we need to be able to recall data that is stored in the memory, when we require it.

Brain-scientists have located the area in the brain where memory retention takes place. This area is called the hippocampus. The hippocampus stores the bare facts. The amygdala stores the emotional dimensions of those facts. The amygdala makes comparisons between experiences. It adds a personal emotional dimension to the facts. "The hippocampus is crucial in recognizing a face as that of your cousin. But it is the amygdala that adds *you don't really like her.*"[6] "Research shows that the amygdala of a rat can begin a reaction to a sensation in as short a span of time as twelve milliseconds. The longer route from thalamus to neo-cortex and then to amygdala appears to take about twice as long as the direct route from thalamus to amygdala. Measurements and comparisons of that sort have yet to be made in the human brain, but a similar ratio is likely to apply."[7]

Interest plays a major part in memory storage. It enhances attention and concentration. Interest generally focuses on survival, self-preservation, power, glory and pleasure. It may also focus on an ideal or an artistic goal. Interest may stem from love, hope, lust, or appetite. We can state what interest entails and what its aims are. There are certain ingredients that stimulate interest. Yet each case of interest is unique, as unique as the individual.

The imagination plays a significant role in our thinking. We have noted that it takes more than legs to run a race. Without legs the imagination can carry one through a race, and even win it. The imagination can lead a person into states of fear but also into states of euphoria. It embellishes reality. When we dream the imagination is at work. The imagination adds flavour to the monotony of daily living. It often mollifies the intensity of focusing exclusively on the problems of life. It also assists the person's thinking and planning.

The person is a complex being. It is imperative that brain scientists continue to investigate brain functioning in order to eliminate myths and to try to establish facts about the role of the brain in directing the body. It is crucially important, too, for medical science and neurological science, in particular, to continue research into establishing the cause of diseases, the cause of certain types of behaviour and how emotions are excited and controlled.

The active memory operates in the prefrontal cortex. Fear, anxiety and anger affect the active memory. Those who are severely emotionally distressed are unable to co-ordinate their responses and reactions to situations and events. In an emotionally distressed state the person's ability to perform effectively and to learn is reduced or distorted depending on the severity or intensity of the emotional distress. If a psychological assessment is performed on a person under stress the results will be unreliable even by accepted standards. Damage to the brain whether it is congenital or the result of an accident will also have serious consequences with regard to thoughts, feelings, comprehension, communication and behaviour.

The mind and the body work in harmony. Any change in brain functioning will influence how we learn, behave and interact socially. Dr. Jean Ayres' sensory integration theory was developed to explain the relationship between brain functioning and behaviour. This theory suggests that we have more than the five senses that we are familiar with, vision, hearing touch smell and taste. Researchers in this area of sensory integration believe that we have numerous senses. They maintain that we have both internal and external senses. The sense of well-being, for example, is an internal sense.

If there is a problem with one sensory system such that it is unable to extend its neuron cells to connect with other neuron cells this may adversely affect another sensory system. This is known as Sensory Integration Dysfunction (SID) which can produce hyperactivity or distraction. A child with this condition may not be able to calm him/herself or accept consolation in times of distress. S/he may lack purpose, appear disorganised, lack variety in play activities, appear clumsy and display poor balance. Dysfunction in any of the sensory systems or a combination of them may produce those symptoms consequently that child may have poor social skills and lack emotional stability. Because this is not a visible disability the child with SID may be given little attention even neglected or treated unfairly.

Parents may worry about the stigma of their child being labelled with Sensory Integration Dysfunction. This is a natural concern but the child can get help to prevent this condition from becoming a major disability. Appropriate sensory integration treatment can greatly benefit the child. However, this disorder has symptoms that may overlap with Attention Deficit Disorder (ADD) or Attention Deficit Hyperactive Disorder (ADHD). These disorders will require different treatments. The hyperactive child with attention deficit will need reduced stimulation, lights may need to be dimmed and radio and television sounds lowered. That child requires security and comfort through hugs and a quiet hiding place. The quiet less responsive child with attention deficit will benefit from an increase in sensory stimulation such as playground activities, activity games, running, swimming, using a punch bag, a trampoline and gentle roughhousing.

Sensory Integration Dysfunction affects the child's ability to learn and behave in an acceptable manner. It is a neurological disorder. Medicine will not cure it. The underlying problem in processing sensations need to be treated, not just the symptoms. Therapeutic music, appropriate sound levels, suitable light, fresh air and of course nutritional foods or food supplements will supply the brain with the oxygen, nutrients, stimulation and calmness that is needed to treat the disorder. Each child may need an individually designed programme to suit his/her condition. If the symptoms of one of those disorders is a consequence of, or exaggerated by a brain injury parents will find it challenging to cope with their new child.

It is often said that, s/he wasn't the same person after an operation, accident or shock. S/he is behaving totally different to the person we knew previously. I am referring here to more serious disorders than SID, ADD or ADHD but also including those conditions. In saying this we may be defining the person in accordance with behaviour and with our expectations of that person's observable behaviour patterns. We tend to judge a person in terms of personality and that personality is projected through the individual's behaviour: actions, mannerisms, speech or silence.

The personality may change as a result of surgery, brain damage or a serious accident. The mind is categorically different. The thoughts a person harbours and the way that that person thinks has been nurtured from birth and even before birth while in the womb. Conditioning, indoctrination and education are the main contributors to the formation of the person's character and personality. Physical actions, behaviour, mannerisms, speech and body language are manifestations of the person's character and personality.

When we inquire into the question of what has not changed in the event of major brain damage we must first establish if the person can think rationally. Perhaps many of the person's memories of the past have gone. But such memories are only accidental to the person in the first place. They are established through contact with the physical world, via the senses. The empirically measurable aspects of the person including the personality may change even beyond recognition. But, we will be left with the existing human being. The immeasurable potential of the human mind, with its moments of existential anxiety and dread, remains inaccessible.

We cannot see, observe or measure a person's scope and power of imagination or creative ability. In schools there is very little time or space in the curriculum devoted to activities that allow for the expression and the enrichment of the imagination and the creative thinking qualities of the mind. Schools are preoccupied with teaching Mathematics, Languages, Geography, History, Social, Personal, Health care and Environmental studies, Physical Education, Religion, Visual Arts, Music and Science.

There is no time for *day-dreaming* or even for musing over what one has learned or discovered in Mathematics or Science. Religion may mean praying, learning bible stories or learning about the history of one or all religions. Music may involve learning notes, melodies and the lyrics of songs. Teaching and learning the arts often consists of a whole group of children doing the same type of task at the same time. The creative aspect of those subjects is often not afforded the time it deserves in schools.

Howard Gardner attempted to broaden the scope of intelligence. He did not see intelligence in terms of its being the sole, single and supreme driving force of the person. On the contrary he speaks about multiple intelligences. Initially, Gardner suggested that the person possesses seven intelligences; *Linguistic, Visual/Spatial, Body/Kinaesthetic, Musical, Logical/Mathematical, Interpersonal and Intrapersonal.* He later added an eighth, a *Naturalist* intelligence and more recently he proposed a ninth an *Existentialist* intelligence. However, he maintains that there may be more than that awaiting discovery. He allows an open-ended definition of intelligence.

This is a radical and new way of viewing intelligence and it has captured the interest of educationalists and psychologists all over the world. His idea of intelligence has appealed to most people for it mollifies the stigma attached to learning difficulties such as dyslexia and speech disorders. It also gives a tremendous boost in confidence to people who are skilful at football, art, music, woodwork, metalwork, embroidery, interior house design, cooking and a host of other skills, but who may have difficulty with academic subjects such as reading, writing, spelling or mathematics.

To suggest that a person is composed of multiple intelligences makes little sense. A person may have a particular talent or multiple talents, and a wide range of abilities, but each person is a single individual intelligent being. Gardner is correct in saying that many people have unique and distinct aptitudes and abilities. We must endeavour to find each individual's particular abilities and we ought to encourage that person to develop and utilise those talents. The Sensory Integration Dysfunction theory draws attention to how little we know about the operation of the brain, the nervous system and the senses. The multiple intelligence theory similarly points to how little we know about intelligence.

The person is an intelligent being. S/he is not a conglomeration of intelligences. The person has but one mind, one intellect. Each individual person may act differently in similar situations. This depends on the person's intellectual capacity, on his/her nurture: acquired knowledge and lived experience as well as on his/her environmental circumstance. These factors may influence mental processing. The person's intellectual ability will determine his/her capacity to think, create and plan.

We can hardly classify interpersonal and intrapersonal skills as intelligences? One's ability to work with, manipulate if necessary and reason with other people may be a political aptitude. It might even be an acquired ability. Many aptitudes are simply skills. Good kinaesthetic skills, skilful football manoeuvres, for example, could be the result of good brain muscle co-ordination, good coaching and training or a combination of all three. If the skilful footballer looses the power of his legs it would appear as if he has lost that talent or perhaps it remains with him but dormant for the rest of his life on earth.

Gardner's greatest contribution to education and psychology is in getting teachers and psychologists to recognise that individuals are gifted in various and different ways. However, we cannot explain intelligence in terms of talents or skills. Skill is a word associated with the physical world rather than the intellectual world. The word *ability* is perhaps the most appropriate word we have for describing how the level of energy in a source is utilised; How the capacity and intensity of a latent source of power produces effective energy. Gardner may have placed too much emphasis on the physical observable actions and capabilities of the person in his attempt to define intelligence. Intelligence directs actions in the appropriate manner in order to produce propitious human achievements.

Intelligence cannot be equated with skill. Gardner's definition is too broad to mean anything other than that each individual has multiple talents and many people have particular outstanding talents. He sees intelligence in terms of skills. Gardner seems to be aware of this himself but feels that this is acceptable in the context of his vision of teaching and learning.[8]

The question of whether there are different kinds of intelligences is often answered differently by professors of specific fields of research. Jean-Pierre Changeux, a neurobiologist and director of the laboratory of molecular neurology at the institute Pasteur in France, maintains that the concept of intelligence is meaningless as it refers to creativity, analysis, reasoning and perception and it is obvious that all this is mostly a result of education.[9] Daniel Schacter, a psychologist and professor in the department of psychology at Harvard University, believes that there is more than one kind of intelligence.[10]

David Servan-Schreiber, a medical doctor and practicing psychiatrist, believes that EQ (Emotional Intelligence) is more important than IQ. He maintains that the most successful people are those who can interact best with people. Knowledge is less valuable than how to relate to people, to work with a team produces better results than to work as an individual no matter how intelligent the individual may be.[11] Yet, as we know, most of the great works of art, compositions in music and literature, inventions and discoveries have been produced not by teams but by individuals. Perhaps there is a misunderstanding here between creativity and the enactment of creativity. Many creative ideas cannot be affected by the person who created them. It may fall to others to realize the creative idea.

Both Goleman's and Gardner's theories view human intelligence from the physical/material perspective. Others have attempted to explain intelligence in evolutionary terms. Jean Piaget, a developmental psychologist is one of those. He tried to explain intelligence through natural growth and development.[12] Growth and development are dependent on, and connected to the material world, the world of physics. Piaget's developmental theory of the mind maintains that intelligence develops in four stages. He was concerned with the development of intelligence itself more than with the intellectual development of the person. He saw a universal order in things and believed that everything has a relationship to everything else.

For Piaget biological processes and mental processes are similar: How the intelligence functions and develops is biological, he maintained, just as biological in its functioning as digestion or breathing. Piaget viewed the development of intelligence as part of the evolution of the human race. Knowledge and intelligence were just different sides of the same coin. To inquire into knowing is to inquire into intellectualising. This view differs from how epistemologists and psychologists view knowledge and intelligence. For them knowledge applies to facts. Intelligence applies to mental age.

The first stage in intellectual development, according to Piaget, is the *Sensorimotor* stage which lasts from birth to two years. This, he maintained, can hardly be classified as a stage of thought at all; for all real thought only starts at the concrete operations stage. It is not till the concrete operational stage that the child's thinking displays a system of logic. At the first stage, the environment is in complete control. It is the change or evolution from that state to where thought becomes autonomous that characterises Piaget's stages of intellectual development. Piaget believed that the new-born infant cannot think, but the infant is born with a capacity to learn from experience, which leads to and eventually ends with the ability to think.

The second stage of intellectual development lasts from the age of two years to seven years. This stage is divided into two periods – *Preconceptual* or Symbolic period, two to four years, and, *Intuitive* or *perceptual* period four to seven years. In the pre-conceptual period the child develops the ability to represent a thing (which is not present) either through language or through other symbols. Henceforth the child is not constrained by or confined to the immediate environment and the present.

At the perceptual stage the child can give reasons for what s/he does and for what he/she believes. The child now appears to contradict her/himself but from the child's own perspective this is not the case. This is because the child cannot concentrate on, or keep in mind, more than one thing at a time. At this stage the child forgets what went previous to the present thought.

The next stage is the *Concrete Operational* stage. It lasts from seven to twelve years. At this stage the child can deal with more than one operation at a time. Piaget uses the term concrete operations because these operations relate to objects that are concrete rather than to hypotheses outlined in language, which come at the next stage. At the concrete operations stage the child develops the ability to deal logically with objects that are present. This is so because s/he has now developed the ability to classify and serialise. The child can understand substance, weight, volume, area, velocity.

Finally, we have the *Formal Operations* stage, which extends from twelve to fifteen years. During the concrete operations stage the child cannot understand abstract relations independent of content. At this stage the young adult may become concerned with hypothetical relationships and the non-present. Inductive and deductive reasoning develop at this time. Formal thinking is characterised by hypothesis testing. At this stage the person acquires the ability to reason with propositions about data rather than simply dealing with the data as presented.

Most language theorists and psychologists are in agreement that language contributes to the development of thought. According to Piaget language contributes to the development of thought when the formal operations stage has arrived and not before that. Not till this stage will the person employ logical operations in language. Piaget seemed to be of the opinion that from the pre-operational stage language begins to increase the powers of thinking. Wittgenstein, as we have seen maintained that language and thinking is one and the same thing.

Many contemporary psychologists and educationalists believe that thinking precedes language development. If this is true it has profound implications for the appropriate time to teach a language, particularly with regard to the right time to teach reading and writing. Proponents of this viewpoint maintain that opportunities to develop thinking should precede the teaching of reading in particular. Piaget seems to think that thinking and language can be separated. His philosophy is centred on the biological nature of intelligence. He maintained that intelligence develops with education and experience. I do not believe that we can separate language and thinking in this way?

Teaching language is teaching thinking. Children must have sufficient language or thinking ability before they start to read and write; otherwise they will become frustrated with their inability to comprehend what they read assuming that they have mastered the mechanics of reading. The same applies to writing. For writing to have a meaning beyond scribbles on a page the child must have basic thinking ability.

Overt language forms a bridge between the physical and the mental world, between the material and the spiritual.[13] In order to assess a person's intellectual ability we look at the achievements that are a consequence of his/her intellectual reasoning. This is why psychologists and psycho-analysts base a person's intellectual ability on their ability to comprehend and communicate in oral and written language. However, there is an unpredictable dimension to a person, something that is unquantifiable. We cannot measure a person's creative unconscious thoughts.

I do not wish to condemn psychological or psycho-analytical testing but merely to draw attention to their limitations and to guard against the grading of an individual human being's intelligence. We must not place a person on a particular scale as a result of a test devised and administered by another human being. Grading in this way allows the composer of the test the unlawful privilege of being able to grade others in accordance with his/her own standards, beliefs or assumptions. However, this does not prevent us from seeking an understanding of human intelligence.

We need a definition of intelligence if we are to understand the human person. If a word is used regularly by people and the concept denoted by that word cannot be defined, then the word is meaningless. We encounter a communication problem if we are faced with a word or concept that is vague and indefinable. A concept that is understood and has a universally acceptable meaning ought to be articulated and defined in language.

A comprehensive definition of objects in the material world must take account of the elementary composition of the object. It will also include its properties. A comprehensive definition of a living creature ought to take account of its functioning capabilities, its purpose in life vis-a-vis the balance of nature and its material and physical composition. With regard to terms denoting abstract concepts we expect the definition to take account of the meaning as commonly accepted, understood and articulated in its everyday usage.

We have concepts like **nothingness** and **infinity** that are difficult to comprehend. Yet we have arrived at definitions that are satisfactory and enable us to comprehend those concepts. *Nothingness* is the absence of being. If we say that *there was nobody there*, we know very well that there is no such being as *nobody*. But in uttering those words we understand that *nobody* means the absence of a person or body. Similarly, we cannot understand fully the concept *infinity* but we know that it means having no finite bounds, no limits or end. An understanding of the concept requires a comprehension of what it means to have limits and what it means to be finite.

Let us take a brief look at the concepts of *time* and *space*. At the outset, and in order to proceed with any sort of definition, we relate these concepts to ourselves. Those concepts have a metaphysical context but we contextualize them from an existential human perspective. Time involves movement. The universe, the earth and all beings, animate and inanimate are constantly changing. They are never static. We measure time according to how other moving beings affect us, our lives, and our position in space. The movement of the earth around the sun gives us day and night, light and darkness, seasons, growth and decay, cold and heat, and, weather conditions. Our movement in space, our growth, our ageing process are all in harmony with the movement of the earth and universal forces. The earth's movement around the sun gives us a basis for the system of measurement that we call time.

We understand *space* in a similar way. We occupy a space. We can move around only because other beings don't occupy all the space around us. Yet we are restricted in our movements because of other objects and beings. We cannot occupy the same space as a tree, a building or a mountain, nor can we occupy the same space as another living creature, a horse, a dog or a person unless that living creature vacates the space. We understand the vastness of space because we realize that we can never reach the end of unoccupied space or even see the limits of space. Time and space, have a meaning only in relation to me, to my movement and to my location.

Commonly accepted meanings of words make communication possible and fluid.

If we are ever to arrive at any understanding of the mind we must, in the first instance, be capable of distinguishing ourselves categorically and definitively from other animals on the earth. We must, then, see ourselves and others as individual members of the human race. The one who sees the person as but another creature of the animal world can easily produce a definition or description of the human being. The person is an animal with a superior brain, a well-developed cortex and a neo-cortex that can use and comprehend language. Those who see the human being as more than just another animal may define the person as a being with a mind that is intelligent, unique and unparalleled, a being with a brain that is superior to other creatures, a being that can use language but also a being with a physical body that functions in a similar manner to many other animals on earth.

What is this intellectual capacity that distinguishes the human person from other animals? Primates have two legs and two hands quite like humans. The arms and hands are but two other limbs that we use for purposes other than for walking or for moving around. The monkey, the ape and the chimpanzee also use their front limbs to pick up things, to feed themselves and to gesticulate. The human being has developed those two limbs to a higher level but this development alone hardly distinguishes humans from primates. It is the person's ability to create, invent, reason, think and use language to communicate not simply for survival purposes but also in an abstract way that distinguishes the human being from other animals on earth.

The Greek philosopher, Heraclitus saw reason as the driving force of the person. He believed that there is a kind of universal reason that is common to all members of the human race, something that everybody is guided by. Plato a hundred years later made a distinction between the material, tangible world, and the world of ideas. He believed that all material substances dissolve. Material things erode with the passage of time, but an idea has a timeless *form* that is eternal and immutable. All cats, for example, have an identifiable *form*, irrespective of their colour or size. A particular cat will die, but the *form* of the cat is eternal and immutable, and, that which is eternal and immutable cannot be a physical substance. Plato concluded that a reality exists beyond the material world. This reality is the world of ideas. We cannot have true knowledge of things for they are in a constant state of change. Nothing in the world that we perceive with our senses lasts so we can have opinions only about such things.

Plato maintained that we have inaccurate conceptions of what we perceive with our senses but we have true knowledge of what we understand with our reason. We cannot identify a colour with absolute certainty. It may be a lighter or darker shade of the true colour, but we can say with certainty that a right angle has 90° or a triangle has 180°. Plato believed that we have an immortal soul. This soul is not a material substance. It exists in the world of ideas.

According to Plato the soul existed before it entered the body. As soon as the soul enters a body it forgets all the perfect ideas. But as time goes on the person discovers the many *forms* in the natural world. One sees a tree or a cat, but an imperfect tree or cat, the sight awakens in the soul a recollection of the perfect tree or cat that the soul once knew in the world of ideas, this makes the soul wish to return to its true world. Plato called that longing *Eros* (love). The soul longs to return transported by love to the world of ideas. It wishes to be freed from the entanglement of the body. Of course there are people who wish to cling to the material, physical world, a world that is but a shadow of the real world of ideas.

If we see a moving shadow we know that something is causing the shadow. We look and see a horse, for example, something with colour and shape, it is tangible and emits a scent and produces sounds. According to Plato all material things are but shadows of the eternal true forms or ideas. The majority of people are happy to live in a shadow world. They rarely give a thought to what is causing the shadows. They believe that shadows are all that exist. In **The Republic** Plato tells us of what could happen if we lived in a world of shadows. He presents us with an example of a person who lived all his life in a cave seeing nothing of the outside world but shadows of people passing by, reflected on a wall. After spending almost his entire lifetime in the cave that person is freed and walks out into the real world. He now believes that he is in a false world. He wants to return to the cave, his real world.

When Rene Descartes pronounced *Cogito, ergo sum, ergo, sum res cogitans,* he defined the person as *a thinking being*. Like Plato and Socrates, Descartes maintained that knowledge is attainable only through the mind. He mistrusted the senses.

St. Augustine believed that God created the world. The idea was in the divine mind. Augustine saw the Platonic eternal ideas as God's ideas.

Plato held that what we understand with our reason is more real than anything we obtain through our senses. Descartes held a similar view. The thinking 'I', therefore, is more real than the physical world that we sense with our senses. Like Plato, Descartes believed in the duality of the person, we think and we occupy physical space. Descartes maintained that while the mind is not a part of the brain it is linked to the brain through a gland, the pineal gland. This gland is not one of a pair as are other glands and lobes of the brain.

According to Descartes, in this pineal gland, constant interaction takes place between the spiritual and material worlds. Through this interaction the mind is influenced by feelings that relate to the body's needs. But the mind can divorce itself from bodily impulses or drives and operate independently of the material body. We can operate at a level above and beyond our bodily needs and desires through thinking and reasoning.

Descartes separated the mind from the body but awarded the mind a priority over the body. He did not define the mind, or, say what it is, or what it does. Establishing its existence is an important step in its definition. Some things are defined by what they do, by their movement or actions in time and space. The thinking dimension of the person, the mind, might fall broadly into that category but its definition goes beyond what it does and extends into what it is capable of doing, its potential. The intellect has a characteristic that operates outside time and space, that characteristic is the imagination. The mind is ever active; processing, planning, imagining, reminiscing, creating, choosing and judging. Most contemporary theorists and an even greater majority of contemporary scientists have dismissed Descartes' reasoning. Their dismissal has resulted in a failure to develop an understanding of the mind.

J.P. Sartre's existentialist philosophy, continued along the lines of Descartes' thinking. In *Being and Nothingness*, he prioritizes the thinking dimension of the person. Existentialism focuses attention on human consciousness. The person thinks and is conscious. This constitutes human existence. In Existentialist philosophy consciousness is the '*sum*' that Descartes established. The person is not controlled by the material world. Each person chooses his/her own destiny. We are beings with responsibility. We are compelled to choose; even refusing to choose is to make a choice. When we make a choice in life it should not be a random choice, one that we hope will turn out right. We are responsible for our decisions. In this choosing and taking responsibility we are creating and forming our essence which can be defined only after death.

In BEING AND NOTHINGNESS *an essay on phenomenological ontology*[14], Sartre maintained that the person is a hole in being, a negation of being. He is referring here to the person's mind. Sartre is right in saying that the person's mind cannot be defined at any precise moment of time in life. He may not be correct in suggesting that after death this aspect of one's being can be defined or charted. This suggestion indicates that the person's mind dies with the body. We accept that the brain, the empirically observable dimension of our being, ends at death, but, there is no proof that the mind ends there.

We cannot observe a person's thinking. It is elusive. Its very existence is fleeting. It is similar to Heraclitus's person in the river. We cannot stand in the same river twice. The second time we step into that river all the water will have changed. The main constituent of the river is water. Consequently, we are standing in a river that has changed fundamentally. The original water has passed on. Even while standing in the river, instantaneously the water is moving on. We don't have sufficient time to utter the words before the change has taken place.

Thinking is continuous, changing and progressive. In existentialist philosophy this is what constitutes the person's existence. Sartre maintained that at death the person's consciousness ceases to function, *ergo,* the person ceases to exist. He sees consciousness as the person's existence. Existentialism sees the supremacy of the mind over the physical body. Yet Sartre and many other existentialists seem to allow the material world and the physical body to perform the final act, to be the ultimate terminator of the mind.

According to Sartre the mind comes into being when the person is born, it exists and lives with the person and it dies when the person dies. An individual human existence is created by a person's daily thinking and choosing, and, his/her acting in accordance with that thinking and choosing. We are constantly, all through life, involved in the making of ourselves. At death we are made. This is absurd; all through our lives we seek fulfilment, an essence. Then, at death our non-existence allows us to have that essence.

Perhaps we might ask the question: Is the flow of ideas from generation to generation more than an etching on a stone to be interpreted by succeeding generations? We find a stone with scratch marks, art work, drawings etc., it dates back five thousand years. We retreat, pause and interpret. The interpretation may cause the ideas of its author or authors to live again. Thoughts or ideas that are forgotten, lost or buried can be resurrected in this way. They may thus continue to live in another time and place.

Through the study of history, archaeology, philosophy and anthropology we tap into the intellectual existence of our ancestors. We want to get into their thinking, to live in their time and place. Let us take the great megalithic burial tombs at New Grange, Knowth and Dowth in County Meath, a short distance from Dublin, as examples.

We are in awe at the ingenuity of those who constructed these magnificent tombs. We wonder in amazement at the enormous strength, craftsmanship and architectural brilliance of those people who were comparatively small in stature. Above the entrance to the New Grange tomb there is an opening. A huge bolder closed the entrance. The opening over the entrance was deliberately made there to allow the sun's rays to enter and penetrate the inner chamber on mid winter's day. The aperture is small. It must have taken years of planning and observing the light of the sun to achieve this.

The passage is nineteen metres long. It is narrow less than a half metre wide in places and only about one and a half metres in height. Yet its builders without the aid of compasses, modern engineering mathematical equipment, computers or calculators were able to construct with precision a monument with an aperture on a location on the crust of the earth in perfect alignment between the rays of the sun and the inner chamber on a specific day of the year and time of day, the winter solstice at nine o'clock in the morning, the time the sun rises over the Boyne valley. We wonder in awe at how those people succeeded in realizing their goal, how they managed to transport the huge boulders up the hill and to set them in place. How did they lift the enormous cap stone and place it on top of the tomb? No rain enters the tomb, not even in the worst rain storms.

Knowth, another awe inspiring megalithic tomb in the Boyne valley, is constructed in such a way that the sun's rays shine through the main entrance at dawn on the morning of the vernal equinox. At evening sun set on the same day the sun's rays shine through the rear entrance. This happens again on the morning and evening of the autumnal equinox; a truly magnificent planning and engineering achievement. It required patient, continuous record keeping and diligent observation.

These constructions are awesome. We want answers, an explanation. Interpretations have varied but a very credible interpretation seems to be that our early ancestors built New Grange monument to symbolise a pregnant earth. In the dead and darkness of mid-winter, when the Earth is barren and dormant, the sun sends its rays of light and warmth through the aperture and down the passage to impregnate this slumbering planet. This gives rise to new life which develops and grows through the Spring and Summer seasons. Perhaps the souls of the dead were meant to be given new life in this way too. Nine months later on or around the Autumnal equinox the Earth gives birth. Fruits, grain and root crops are ripe and ready to sustain and nourish all creatures on Earth.

We live for a while with our ancestors. We think, dream, wonder and dwell with them. We live through their successes, joys and happiness. We also experience their existential pain. We tune into the minds of the departed souls of our ancestors. We interpret their art and architecture; arousing, penetrating, stimulating and bringing them to new life, in the same way as the sun's rays penetrates and impregnates the dormant Earth at dawn on mid winter's day awaking it from its slumbers and giving it new life.

ENDNOTES:

CHAPTER V

[1] See CHAPTER I

[2] Goleman, Daniel **EMOTIONAL INTELIGENCE** First Published 1996 – paperback edition 1996 Bloomsbury publishing, 38 Soho Sq, London WIV 5D.F. p. 20

[3] John Anderson Secrets of the MIND, CD ROM, Focus

[4] Robert Plutchick Secrets of the MIND

[5] Goleman, Daniel **SOCIAL INTELLIGENCE** First published by Arrow Books 2007 p. 128

[6] Goleman, Daniel **EMOTIONAL INTELLIGENCE** p 20 Goleman quotes what Le Doux once said to him.

[7] Ibid. p.21

[8] Armstrong, Thomas **MULTIPLE INTELLIGENCES.** p.3

[9] Jean-Pierre Changeux - Secrets of the MIND, CD ROM, Focus

[10] Schacter, Daniel - Secrets of the MIND, CD ROM, Focus

[11] Servan-Schreiber, David - Secrets of the MIND, CD ROM, Focus

[12] Piaget, J. **THE ORIGIN OF INTELLIGENCE IN THE CHILD,** translated by Margaret Cook – first publ. in English 1953 by Rutledge, Keegan Paul – London and Henley - 4th impression.

[13] See CHAPTER 2

[14] Sartre, J.P **BEING AND NOTHINGNESS**, an essay on; Phenomenological Ontology Published by Methuen, London 1969

CHAPTER VI

EDUCATION, WISDOM & IQ
Teach the body, heed the mind

The mind is ever active organizing our world for us. The conscious mind attends to our material welfare in the world, our survival, evolutionary development, social interactions, needs and appetites. The unconscious mind operates at a higher level, creating, planning and sorting out the difficulties we encounter and the problems we become embroiled in every day. Educators ought to set aside time to allow the mind freedom to dream. The relaxed mind is creative. "Sometimes your intelligence may oppose your immediate desire because it knows the long term consequences. Thus, the role of intelligence is to determine the positive and negative potential of an event or factor which could have both positive and negative results. It is the role of intelligence, with the full awareness that is provided by education, to judge and accordingly utilize the potential for one's own benefit or well-being."[1]

The creative potential of the mind is often inhibited by our preoccupation with material things. We should devote more time and attention to the mental/spiritual aspect of our being. This may involve allowing dream-time in schools, to give the unconscious mind an opportunity to compose, invent and create. Spiritual education liberates the mind and detaches it from the material world. The mind should be actively involved in the learning process, too. The child needs time to dream but also time to explore and discover. Achieving our goals as teachers and learners requires analytical thinking. We teach children to analyse acquired information so that as they mature they become masters of their own destiny.

Child centred education should take precedence over didactic teacher-centred methods in teaching and learning. Education, in its broadest sense, caters for the development of all aspects of the human person. Analysis helps to bridge the gap between the intellectual world and the material world. Analytical thinking and philosophy ought to be included in primary and second level curricula. Thinking critically about what is happening in the world around us is essential. This includes critical analysis of advertisements and political statements. Education, by and large, evolves and develops to suit changing environments and circumstances. Through the development of overt and subliminal sophisticated marketing strategies and the huge expansion of available information, the danger of consumer exploitation leaves the children of today less protected than were their predecessors

In teacher centred education the teacher teaches, the child listens. The traditional approach saw the teacher and the textbooks as the initiators and conveyors of all that was taught. The inculcation and reinforcement of information was considered more important than analysis of presented data. A rigid teacher driven didactic method of teaching is unacceptable today but so too is progressive education in the pragmatic sense where teaching and learning are of value only if practical and useful results are produced.

'Pragmatism', as a philosophy of education, made the mistake of limiting knowledge to personal experience, and to one's own interpretation of the world. John Dewey asks us to: "Abandon the notion of the subject matter as something fixed and ready-made in itself, outside the child's experience."[2] Dewey's conclusion that education is purely a social phenomenon is hardly correct. The person must be conscious of social obligations but s/he must also develop as a thinking, critical and responsible individual.

Activity methods of teaching have focused on ways to develop and improve sensation and perception. Montessori, Kilpatrick, Froebel, Dewey and many others emphasised the importance of developing the child's perceptual awareness through activity methods. These methods see the child rather than the teacher as the central figure in teaching and learning. Child-centred education involves the child directly in his/her own learning. The use of the senses in activity work awakens and sharpens perceptual awareness and discrimination. In teacher centred education some of the senses may receive little or no stimulation.

We should encourage children to listen more attentively to various sounds. Auditory discrimination ought to be more to the fore in teaching and learning. From an early age children should be taught to listen to the sounds of nature; water-falls, wind, sea waves beating against cliffs. The sense of touch has been grossly neglected in teaching until recently. Differentiating between different materials; fabrics, liquids and solids essential in primary classroom learning

The sense of smell is neglected most of all. This sense is hardly even referred to in an educational context, yet, many animals depend on this sense for survival. We have organised our world such that we rarely need this sense or so we might think. Yet, in the case of fire we smell the burning material and the smoke usually before we hear, feel or see the fire. If there is a gas leak in a building we generally detect it through smell. If we are given something harmful to eat we may first react to the smell of the food. If it smells good we want to eat it. If it smells bad we reject it.

Children should be better educated to detect various odours. Identifying the scent of various flowers, fruits, vegetables, herbs, trees, wood, turf, heather and various shrubs should be included in classroom teaching. Children might be educated to differentiate between the aromas of various trees, plants, fruits etc: pine and furze, roses and carnations, tomatoes and cucumbers, pears and apples, peat and upland. They should be taught to actively and consciously smell them and other aromas too. It is not sufficient for children to be just passively aware of odours.

The taste sense is educated naturally in the home and in society generally. Nevertheless, teaching children to describe and compare tastes could be beneficial. We could ask children to differentiate between the taste and texture of apples and pears, for example. Pupils might be asked to distinguish and identify the flavour of strawberries, raspberries, cherries, pineapples, lemons and melons. We haven't even developed appropriate language to describe tastes. Could we describe and compare the taste and texture of carrots, peas, potatoes, tomatoes and turnips? Educating the taste sense might help people to enjoy foods, to be more discriminatory in choosing foods and to avoid over eating, particularly of unhealthy foods.

In the primary school, the art programme helps to educate the sense of sight. Music educates the hearing sense. The art lesson may need to focus more on colour. Colour discrimination must focus on the variations of the primary colours, how light and shade effect colour. Pupils might be taught to appreciate colour co-ordination, colour contrast, design and blends of colours. They should be taught to appreciate sounds; harmony, beat and rhythm. They should learn to tune in to changes in sounds. This is an important life skill. We should develop good listening habits and not expect passive hearing to come to our defence in times of crisis.

Children of today spend too much time gazing at a television screen or playing computer games and not enough time in actively discovering and exploring their environment and the world beyond them. Many children also eat an inordinate amount of soft, junk food and fizzy drinks. If humans do not use their teeth they will lose them. Evolution will see to it that if teeth are not required for chewing food children will shed them early in life and the second set will not develop or humans may remain toothless from birth.

Darwin showed how finches changed the shape of their beaks in accordance with what and how they ate food. A similar consequence could befall any human faculty or skill if it is not used, neglected or no longer required. In the future this could apply to the skills of reading, writing and spelling. The same applies to an over dependency on calculators to the neglect of learning tables and basic mathematical formula. Rote learning is useful so long as the learner understands the concept and the method of calculating.

We must learn to discover. We must also learn facts about our world. Spending too much time gazing at a computer screen and watching events unfold may leave children unable to discriminate between fact and fiction. " For the first time in human history, individuality could be obliterated in favour of a passive state, reacting to a flood of incoming sensations – a 'yuck' and 'wow' mentality characterized by a premium of momentary experience as the landscape of the brain shifts into one where personalised brain connectivity is either not functional or absent altogether."[3] Susan Greenfield, a brain scientist, believes that playing computer games boosts the chemical dopamine in the nucleus accumbens, one of the brain's pleasure centres, which is linked to the prefrontal cortex.

Too much dopamine may reduce activity in the prefrontal cortex, distorting a child's awareness of the meaning of their actions. The human brain will react to changes.[4] "It is exquisitely malleable; a significant alteration in our environment and behaviour has consequences."[5] Educators may need to counteract the harmful effects on children of excessive television gazing and computer or other electronic type game playing by encouraging greater interpersonal communication and greater use of the senses to discover and increase awareness of the world outside them.

No single theory of teaching and learning is powerful enough to account for all that goes on within the classroom. Consequently, the search for a panacea to suit all situations, in the area of method, is a futile exercise. However, most contemporary educationalists accept that the child-centred activity approach should be among every good teacher's repertoire of methods. This was the method that our early ancestors used to educate themselves before the establishment of formal schools.

Despite the great advances in the area of activity methods, promoted by Rousseau, Fitzpatrick, Dewey, Froebel, Montessori and many others, in recent years these methods appear to have been diluted or even discarded and the traditional approach reintroduced. Yet, no matter what attempts are made to turn back the clock, purposeful activity methods have focused attention on the child as the central figure in education. This, in turn, has led to the introduction of learning support, resource help and specialist teaching for children who find it hard to learn and those with specific learning difficulties.

The child, though an individual, feels the need to belong to a group. We can channel this need and use it to the child's advantage. During the early adolescent years students will accept the authority of their own peers more readily than that of a teacher. They may not be interested in the teacher's efforts to encourage a critical attitude to all they hear, see and learn. They may want to follow a cult, a fashion or a peer-led linear way of thinking. The teacher need not be discouraged by this. Group project work at this stage in the student's life will help to develop independence as well as social interaction and cooperation. Child centred activity methods of education allow the student to become directly involved in his/her own learning and in the case of group projects to be socially involved while doing so.

Child centred education necessitates that work programmes be arranged in order to benefit every child, taking account of each individual's stage of development, ability level, acquired skills and interests. The teacher who teaches with conviction and with an effective method will realize his/ her goals. Enthusiasm radiates from the teacher who believes in the subject matter being taught and the inherent worth of that subject matter to each child. It is important to critically analyse the content of all information taught. If a teacher believes strongly enough in the philosophy that s/he teaches then aspiring towards the ideals of that philosophy will become a dream, a dream that s/he will be keen to achieve. As well as having a philosophy a teacher also needs a method to impart the ideals of that philosophy. A group activity method with the key elements *direction, research, experience, analysis and mediation (DREAM)* might be a useful method in seeking this objective.

Group project work is most suited to the age bracket nine to fifteen years and the ideal and most manageable number of students involved in a group project is five. A leader will need to be appointed from among the group. The teacher, leader and other members of the group decide on the role of each member of the project team. The end result might contain a display chart or model display and an accompanying booklet. The chart or model display should be visually informative, similar to an advertising poster. It ought not contain a lot of words. Effective colouring, appropriate visual art work or photographs, large bold-faced writing, and, the layout will determine the pedagogical success of the display. Ongoing assessment is also necessary and critical analysis is vital on the completion of the project work.

Selected or volunteering pupils from within the group might choose or be assigned various tasks such as researching and collecting information from the local public library, from encyclopaedias, the internet or from relevant agencies through written / e-mail correspondence. This information will be the data for the booklet. Surveys and statistics should be included where possible in order to give credibility to the work and to intensify and broaden students' interests and participation.

One member could be given responsibility for typing or handwriting the booklet, another for the art-work and chart display, the leader edits the material in consultation with the group and helps to direct the research. The teacher encourages the group to conduct their own research and directs them towards finding relevant information. They research, explore and discover. They experience success and sometimes failure. Learning to cope with failure is as valuable as coping with success. Critical analysis is the key to editing data. The group leader, with assistance or direction from the teacher will analyse the data collected from group members and discard irrelevant material.

The final stage involves a briefing or demonstration by the group to their colleagues on their findings and illustrated work. Classmates ought to be given the opportunity to respond, criticise and give their own personal views on the substance and content of the presentation. A main spokesperson is appointed who will be the mediator of the group. However, each member will be expected to contribute during this presentation stage. The communication, discussion and demonstration of the work involving the project team and the class of students should improve pupils' communicative skills and prepare them for public speaking or leadership roles in later life. It will also broaden and sharpen their vocabulary and improve their ability to speak clearly, accurately and concisely.

Communicating with class colleagues in this way will reinforce for each individual what has been researched and it will improve attention, retention and recall. Through this oral communication and pupil participation students will learn to applaud achievement, tolerate the less successful and criticise constructively. This mediation dimension with its participative, analytical and critical approach has been neglected, by and large, in both the traditional and activity methods of teaching,

Young people are needed for leadership roles in all aspects of life. They will be required to analyse marketing strategies, publicity inducements and soliciting, and, to have the ability and confidence to voice their criticism publicly and communicate it in written form too. In doing this they will need to be able to present facts and figures as well as point to their source of information. They will also need to be capable of interpreting statements, comments and hypotheses. Furthermore, it is important that they learn to analyse interpretations and opinions. It is not sufficient to assert the truth of an argument or statement simply by claiming to have heard or read that it is true. Every effort must be made to ensure that interpretation is founded and grounded on evidence, experience and on sound, solid logical inferences in order to give it credibility. Finally, when this demonstration and class participation, involving questions, comments, suggestions and analysis is completed, the work will be suitably located for display in the classroom, the library or a selected area of the school.

An important aspect of education is awareness of the crucial distinction between knowledge and propaganda, and, the adoption of steps to ensure that knowledge acquired will help to advance the educational philosophy pursued. Consequently, it is imperative that we include ongoing analysis in all activity methods. A great deal of analysis is carried out by the mind, unconsciously, but a substantial amount of conscious critical analysis is also essential in educational practice. If we fail to get pupils to think critically about what they are doing and learning we are failing in our mission as educators.

Traditional and contemporary educators, too, are mainly concerned with educating the child's mind. Children sit in a classroom and are taught through text books or standard lessons projected on a screen. Teaching and the school system focus attention on children's minds. Psychologists, counsellors and teachers assume or are given roles to assess and educate the child's mind. The theory is that in educating the mind we will improve and sharpen the operation of the senses.

In the not too distant past educators held the view, and many teachers today hold the same view that doing complex exercises, even if one does not comprehend them, sharpens and develops the mind. Difficult mathematical problems and rote learning keep the mind active and might be compared with how physical exercise and gymnastics benefit the body, according to those who subscribe to that belief. This may not be correct but there is a lot of merit in rote learning when the content being learned by heart is understood by the student. In teaching and learning a certain amount of rote learning should be encouraged.

It seems strange that a person advocating the primacy of the mind would promote the education of the senses and encourage activity methods of teaching in preference to conventional mind centred teaching. It seems just as strange that those who see the priority of the material world over the mind should promote methods of teaching that are directed almost exclusively at educating the mind while neglecting activity methods that put more emphasis on sense experience.

There is no contradiction here for those who see the primacy of the mind over material reality. The apparent contradiction can be explained if we appreciate the valuable role of sense experience in *responsive thinking*[6]. The more sense experiences and knowledge we obtain the more data we have to think on. Activities involving sense experience may also involve thinking. The mind and body work in harmony for the most part.

We must ask the question; are those who have acquired little or no sense experiences less able to think than those with lots of sense experience, and consequently, are they less intelligent? This is a key question, for if the mind depends totally on sense experience then it is dependent on the material world for its existence. Such a conclusion could close the argument concerning the essence of the mind. Perhaps a superficial metaphysical debate would continue. This is what has happened to a large extent. Contemporary society is directed by and accepts science, with its technological methodologies and discoveries, as the arbiter of truth. Few people are concerned about teasing out this question more comprehensively with the possibility of arriving at an alternative conclusion.

There is no contradiction in accepting that the mind draws information from the outside world via the brain and the senses while at the same time accepting that the world impinges on the senses and as a result affects thinking. The senses, in themselves, cannot make sense of what they sense. Sensing and sensations are categorically different to reasoning and rationality. The word experience presupposes a flow of information from a material world to an intellectual world. In speaking of *an experience* we have gone beyond the stage of experiencing and are reflecting on some particular experience. It is accepted as an experience (only) when conscious awareness of it has taken place. Accumulated experiences and information lead to knowledge acquisition and knowledge with the aid of analysis leads to wisdom. Experiencing has its source in the material world, for the most part, although one can have a spiritual or intellectual experience too. The raw material for thinking may come from the material world but the operation of thinking itself is quite different. It is not physical in the way that walking, breathing and digesting are physical acts.

Psychology is a science that humans have developed in order to try to understand how people think and to measure their level of intelligence. Yet psychologists are reluctant to give a definition of intelligence. Dictionary definitions are too general and too vague. The Oxford dictionary defines intelligence as "quickness of understanding, sagacity."[7] The same dictionary gives the meaning of an *intelligence quotient* as the number denoting the ratio of a given person's intelligence to the norm or average. An intelligence test, according to that dictionary, is designed to measure intelligence rather than to measure acquired knowledge. Intelligence is often defined too, as the way in which creatures perform in order to overcome obstacles.

Psychological assessments are designed to measure a person's intellectual ability. These tests may measure an individual's ability to perform certain tasks, to calculate, to understand spatial dimension. They may measure knowledge acquired. They may also measure a person's general comprehension of the world pertaining to sight and sight recognition, hearing and sound recognition as well as his/her ability to memorize, retain, recognize and subsequently recall data.

Tests are divided into verbal and non-verbal tasks. They also set out to measure reasoning ability. The skills that they measure, however, are the result of experience acquired in the material world. Of course most psychological tests have a number of sub-tests that aim to test creativity *as well as speed* and sharpness of memory retrieval through recognition. Some tests may require the participant to recognise reflected and reversed words, letters and other commonly used symbols. The person who has experience in such tasks will perform much better than the one who has no experience.

Sigmund Freud tried to understand the mind through an analysis of the person's dreams. Dreams, according to Freud, reveal a person's unconscious desires or repressed thoughts.[8] He maintained that most of our thoughts reside in the unconscious mind. Our expression of thoughts, either through verbal language or behaviour, is the public display of our inner thinking. Most outward expressions of thoughts are expressed for public consumption. From early in life we learn to be tactful, diplomatic and careful in giving a response.

We often hear of the person who 'put his foot in it'. We learn to choose our words and watch our behaviour. We behave like all those people who saw the naked emperor parade through the streets but applauded the new clothes he was wearing. It took an innocent child to voice the truth. In contemporary society there is often little or no credits awarded for such honesty. The person who speaks her mind too freely may lose friends and become ostracised. We learn to conform. In order to be accepted we are expected to portray a certain image. We lose ourselves in the image. We are like the heavily laden ship in the ocean. We see only about a third of the ship, the most polished part, the display. Two thirds remain hidden below water. Our thoughts are the same.

Contemporary psychology endeavours to understand the mind of the person through an observation of that person's overt behaviour. This is no more than an attempt to comprehend the mind through observing the body and it's functioning. Here the impression is given that the body takes precedence over the mind. Descartes' great effort to give the mind a priority status is dismissed. To say that there is nothing in the mind that has not already come through the senses places the mind in a subordinate position to the physical body and the material world. This leaves the mind dependent on the senses. The conclusion from this reasoning is that the mind would not exist without the senses and the senses would have nothing to sense were it not for the external material world. Even neuroscience accepts today that while the vast majority of the cortex is devoted to sensory processing the frontal lobes deal with non-sensory tasks: "The perceptual system does not always agree with the rational thinking cortex." [9]

I think, therefore I am, is one statement that has not come through the senses. To doubt is to think was how Saint Augustine put it. Through doubting I come to the conclusion that *I exist*. Doubting that I doubt is thinking. Doubting is thinking and thinking is proof of the existence of thinking. It is proof of mental processing and reflection. This is not a material or physical existence but a mental existence. To inquire into the concept and meaning of the mind is something that does not come through the senses. It certainly appears plausible to state that the mind can operate independently of the senses. However, we know that the senses provide the data for everyday thinking, i.e. data on the material world. From an educational point of view educating the senses must be given much more prominence than heretofore. We need to understand the material world. It is essential, too, that we give time and thought to the non-material; the mental, the spiritual world.

When psychologists set out to measure a person's intelligence they are measuring the knowledge gained and the experience acquired by the person. They are also setting out to establish or impose restrictions and limits to the person's ability to apply acquired knowledge and experience. Psychological assessments may measure a person's ability to cope in certain circumstances and under certain conditions. It must seem strange to the true materialist, however, to the person who dismisses the mind, that even the physical body, that part of the person that appears to be empirically verifiable can be verified only by a mind, by an intelligent being. Medical remedies for illnesses, organ transplants and recent surgical and biological advances, such as cloning, are planned by an intelligent human being before they are administered, performed or executed.

An idea and plans to execute an idea come from the mind of a person, a scientist, an engineer, an architect, a geneticist. We cannot expect the physical sciences to define, explain or verify the existence of the mind. Those who dismiss the existence, or diminish the importance of the mind, but use that mind to try to prove its non-existence are hardly being logically consistent. Most advances in science and in technology are based on new discoveries and inventions. Heart and lung transplants are a culmination of simple heart surgery and heart transplants. Aircraft are improved and perfected as defects and deficiencies in existing aircraft are observed and repaired. This could lead us to believe that all knowledge comes through experience.

A person's mind cannot be empirically measured. It is not possible to determine scientifically the capacity of the mind. The potential of the human mind cannot be determined. When we consider the many great inventions and creations by individual human beings we will come to realize that the mind is unpredictable. We can guess what a person will do or how s/he will behave under certain circumstances, but, it is only a guess and it can never be scientifically measured. We can measure acquired information to some extent though this too may be difficult to quantify accurately for the person may know more than s/he is able to express, write or type under an examination setting. But, with regard to information it has been acquired or it hasn't. The manner in which information is received depends on its presentation and on the disposition of the person receiving it. A person may fail to acquire particular information due to lack of interest and attention at the time of presentation or due to factors relating to sensation and perception or other difficulties. Even in a case where information is acquired, retrieval may not always be accurate. Some acquired data and information may become lost or buried in the unconscious mind.

What we are doing in information - based examinations is testing the person's ability to perceive, comprehend, remember and how s/he can then express verbally, orally or in writing what s/he has perceived, learned and retained. We could test many animals' ability to learn and produce results in a similar manner.

We cannot measure wisdom, for while wisdom is dependent on

knowledge and experience it is also linked to intelligence. It involves the mind applying knowledge acquired effectively and advantageously to novel situations in varying and unpredictable circumstance. Many people are of the opinion that accumulated experiences lead to knowledge and knowledge leads to wisdom. The knowledgeable and wise people are the leaders in today's world. However, the statement, *accumulated experiences lead to knowledge and knowledge leads to wisdom*, is not an unequivocal truth. Some people may have numerous experiences but may be unable to convert them to knowledge. Others who can convert experiences to knowledge may not use that knowledge, or, they may be unable to use the knowledge acquired, wisely.

We need intelligence to become wise. However, a person may be intelligent but not yet wise. The intelligent person has the potential to become wise. Aristotle pointed out that wisdom comes with age, "a young man of practical wisdom cannot be found,"[10] he said. This is because the older one grows the more experience s/he acquires and consequently, the more knowledge of the world s/he possesses. It would hardly be true to say that intelligence comes with age. Wisdom is acquired. We cannot say that intelligence is acquired. It is the intelligence that converts experience to knowledge and knowledge to wisdom. Wisdom is the result of intelligence and not the other way round. We are born with intelligence but not with wisdom. An indication of the extent of one's responsive thinking is his ability, speed and accuracy in converting experience to knowledge and knowledge to wisdom. The other aspect of intelligence, creative thinking, is more difficult to assess.

Attempts to define a person through an intelligence quotient assessment may be unethical. It may not be fair for one human being to perform an intelligence test on another and consequently, to rate another human being's intellectual ability. It is wrong to attempt to limit the scope of another human being's intelligence or to compartmentalise it. The language used in many psychological assessment reports may not be relevant to the person's intelligence. *He is a tall boy with blue eyes. She has brown hair. She is the second child in a family of four children. He was born with a cleft palate. She has a dimple on her chin. He has a lovely smile.* These sentences are irrelevant in the context of intelligence. They have no bearing on a child's intellectual ability.

Irrelevant too, with regard to intelligence, are statements referring to what a child's mother, father or teacher said: Mother reports that ***Jennifer*** had a *pleasant childhood, a normal birth or a premature birth*. The teacher reports that ***Mary*** *sucks her thumb or displays anger when corrected*. Stating, in the written report what another person has said or observed may be taken as partisan or biased reporting. A lot of this information is valuable but in the context of intelligence such observations and second hand information are irrelevant.

Through random sample surveys it has been observed that children perform better on Intelligent Quotient (IQ) tests if they have eaten certain foods before the test. This may be true, for intelligence though not in the category of material substance, is influenced by the physical/biological body. We may be measuring only certain aspects of intelligence in those tests, aspects that are influenced by the capacity and capability of the brain. We cannot fully divorce the material from the spiritual dimension of intelligence in everyday life. The physical aspect, which is influenced by the brain and the outside material world, is quantifiable to a certain degree but the spiritual dimension is of a different category and is unquantifiable. Psychological assessments cannot measure human intelligence.

I suggest dispensing with the notion of Intelligence Quotient and instead introducing a psycho-behavioural profile. The psycho-behavioural assessment ought to include many of the subtests contained in most of the present psychological assessments such as, memory retention and recall, speed processing, visual and auditory perceptual skills. It should also include some self assessment and assessment on emotional reactions and the person's ability to empathise. There should be an aptitude or skills assessment too, taking account of Gardner's categories of abilities, what he calls multiple intelligences.

In an intelligence assessment report we often read statements like; *this child felt under stress at the time of the assessment, she could not relax, she was very much at ease*, or *he was very giddy*. Here we are accepting that the mood of the individual could influence the result. The question that must be asked then is: To what degree is this assessment report valid in the context of intelligence. Or can that report be accepted at all? It may not always be possible to identify the mood of the person undergoing an assessment for most individuals are capable of hiding or suppressing their moods and emotions in certain circumstances.

No test can measure intelligence adequately. The language expressed orally or in written form, or, the body language of the person under assessment displays or demonstrates the level of acquired knowledge and the behavioural traits of the person, only. In fact, the results may be a poor barometer even of those aspects of the person. The person under assessment may be shy in displaying his/her knowledge and behaviour traits or s/he may exaggerate behaviour.

The mind's being devoid of material substance does not mean that it does not exist. It means only that it cannot be scientifically examined. The physical world that we live in is ever changing. We can see, observe and empirically examine the material world. We can even determine with fine and accurate mathematical calculations the rate, the degree and speed of change. We can take a still picture, as it were, of the material world. We can photograph things. We can x-ray and scan material objects. We can even x-ray and scan the brain and determine how active it is at any given time. We cannot examine the thinking process in that way. Thinking is unpredictable. It is elusive.

Psychology attempts to apply similar or parallel testing methods to mental processes as the physical sciences apply to material being. Psychology sets about measuring intelligence through behaviour observation as it realizes that thinking cannot be measured in the physical sense. Behaviour is seen as the physical display and manifestation of the person's mental existence. However, such observations may be no more than 'Good Guess' work. The whole area of introspection and intellectualising belongs to a category that cannot be examined empirically by scientific methods.

If we refuse to acknowledge the existence of the mind because we cannot empirically examine it we are neglecting, ignoring and dismissing the essential element of our being. Teaching and learning involve the mind absorbing and analysing information for our own benefit both materially and spiritually and for the benefit of the human race. Consequently, it is imperative that we inquire into the existence and the essence of the mind and its modus operandi.

It is necessary, of course, for society to establish norms; to set standards of behaviour as well as lay down minimum limits and acceptable norms with regard to acquired knowledge. However, while establishing those norms and standards may not be too difficult, assessing the level of achievement may be an onerous task. Knowledge and behaviour do not constitute human intelligence? Nor is intelligence a combination of knowledge and behaviour. Knowledge plays a major role in behaviour and behaviour is important in knowledge acquisition.

Acceptable behaviour pertains to all living creatures. Animals possess instinctive behaviour traits. They learn behaviour patterns too, as we do. Animals also acquire knowledge. From the very moment of existence living creatures learn about their environment, the more knowledge they acquire in this regard the higher will be their chances of survival and of having a long and contented life. Predators must learn about the behaviour of their prey and animals being preyed upon must learn about the behaviour of their predators. Acquiring knowledge and adapting behaviour to aid their survival are natural instinctive characteristics of all living creatures.

We humans must acquire knowledge and adapt our behaviour in order to ensure our survival. The purpose of education, according to William James, is to organise the child's thinking and behaviour so that s/he will appreciate and adjust to his/her environment.[11] Contemporary humans may be guilty, not only of neglecting to attend adequately to the education of the mind, but also of neglecting to attend sufficiently to our survival by polluting the land, air and water of our planet. Worse still, contemporary societal structures apparently want to reduce the person to the level of a machine. We hear of *productivity* with regard to intellectual pursuits; in teaching and learning. This notion suggests that we can produce results in the intellectual domain comparable with material processing. We place very little emphasis on teaching metaphysics, philosophy, or the use of the imagination. Those subject areas should be given greater priority in our education system. We should pay more attention to the unconscious mind. Perhaps we should allow the mind to care for the body. Train the body. Teach the brain. Heed the mind.

Conclusion

Bruce Hood in his book 'Super sense' sees the brain as the creator of the mind. "Even though humans have the capacity to reason and make judgements, I think that we will always regard some things in life as not reducible to rational analysis. That is because society needs supernatural thinking as part of a belief system that holds members of a group together by sacred values".[12] This is correct but that may not be the only reason for holding supernatural beliefs. He concludes his book with the question:

"Will humankind ever evolve into the bright species that uses logic over and above emotion and intuition?"[13]

Intelligence is not a battery of information and knowledge nor is it wisdom. Thinking is the essential ingredient of intelligence. Thinking is a continuous stream of mental processing. It is process as opposed to product. An individual cannot decide not to think. Even to think about *nothing* is to think. Intelligence includes the ability to comprehend abstract ideas, and, the ability to make concrete or bring to fruition, ideas and plans.

Intelligence involves an ability to reason logically and to understand other people's logical reasoning as well as the ability to produce original ideas, works of art, music, literature, architecture, engineering etc. Inventions, creations and compositions are the product of intelligence. Masterpieces in art, music, literature as well as scientific inventions and discoveries are the tangible and verifiable results of intellectualisation.

Unlike other animate and inanimate beings the human being is not totally controlled by nature. We can deliberately bring about change and influence natural phenomena. Nature is not the supreme intelligence. Humanity is not the supreme intelligence either. Human intelligence has a creative and a communicative dimension and may be linked to a universal intelligence. It is not unreasonable to believe that a supreme universal intelligence directs and guides evolution. We must not deduce from this, or make the mistake of thinking that education ought to cater only for the intellectual development of the person. In fact it requires the opposite approach.

We educate the physical aspect of the person, primarily. In doing this we give the mind the superior role it deserves. We do not need to be provocative in our approach to the *dialectic tension* between the material and the mental. We educate the whole person keeping in mind that s/he is an *intellectual being* with a material body rather than a body with a mind.

Intelligence is essentially spiritual and unquantifiable. The physical body is essentially material and quantifiable. One of the primary aims of education ought to be the periodic freeing of the mind from earthly attachments. Allow time for the mind to meditate on images beyond the material world. We are privileged to live in a continuous thinking mode.

We are simultaneously condemned to dwell in existential torment through, restless unending thinking. Sum res cogitans.

ENDNOTES:

CHAPTER VI

[1] Dalai Lama THE **DALAI LAMA'S** BOOK OF WISDOM Published byThorsons 1999 p.13

[2] Dewey, John **THE CHILD AND THE CURRICULUM and THE SCHOOL AND SOCIETY** The University of Chicago Press, Chicago and London 1902 – A combined edition 1956, 12th impression 1974 – p.11

[3] Greenfield, Susan, A Sunday Times article by John Cornwell - Sunday April 27th 2008

[4] *Ibid*

[5] *Ibid*

[6] *RESPONSIVE THINKING* – see chapter V - aposteriori thinking

[7] **THE CONCISE OXFORD DICTIONARY** Seventh edition 1982 edited by J.B. Sykes. First ed. 1911 Publ. Oxford Univ. Press p.521

[8] Freud, Sigmund **THE INTERPRETATION OF DREAMS** Translated by James Strachey, published 1991

[9] Carter, R. **MAPPING THE MIND** op. cit., p.194

[10] Aristotle **THE NICOMACHEAN ETHICS** translation of **ETHICA NICOMACHEA** Published 1925 reprint 1969 – London, Oxford Univ. Press p.148

[11] James, W. **THE PRINCIPLES OF PSYCHOLOGY** Vol.1 Publisher: Dover publications 1950 Hood, Bruce op. cit., p.263

[12] Hood, Bruce op. cit., p.263

[13] *Ibid* p.264

GLOSSARY

A POSTERIORI THINKING: *posterior to,* responsive thinking—thinking that depends on sensory data

A PRIORI THINKING: *prior to;* creative thinking—thinking that is independent of sensory data

ACTIVITY METHODS OF TEACHING/LEARNING: Here the learner is actively involved in learning. The teacher oversees the work in progress—learner engages, teacher facilitates.

AMYGDALA: Amygdalae (plural) two almond shaped, and about the size of an almond, brain structures; situated in the right and left temporal lobes. They are part of the limbic system and are the emotional centres of the brain. The Amygdalae process emotional input and often prepare an immediate reaction.

ANALYTHICAL THINKING: analysing information before issuing a response.

ARCHETYPES: Carl Jung's psychoanalytic theory contains nine archetypes by which dreams can be interpreted. They are: *The wise man, the trickster, the shadow, the divine child, the anima, the aminus, the hero, the persona and the great mother.*

ATTENTION DEFICIT DISORDER (ADD): a poor attention span, a person with this condition can be lethargic.

ATTENTION HYPERACTIVE DEFICIT DISORDER (ADHD):
a poor attention span, a person with this condition is hyperactive,
often impulsive, impatient and reactionary.

BROCA'S AREA: the speech area, situated in the frontal lobe, generally
in the left frontal lobe. Discovered by Pierce Paul Broca, a French
Neurosurgeon in 1865

CARTESIAN: relating to the philosopher, Rene Descartes.

CEREBELLUM: a large brain section attached to and tucked
underneath the cerebral hemispheres. It plays a major role in
motor control. It has an involvement in cognitive functions too,
particularly language and attention.

CEREBRUM: This is what we often call the brain. It is situated on
top of the brainstem. The cerebrum controls speech and language
and other human activities; thought, learning, working memory,
judgement and social interactions.

CHILD-CENTRED EDUCATION: Education that sees each child as
the centre of teaching and learning. It contrasts with large group
teaching—here the child takes precedence over the group or class.

COGITO ERGO SUM: Rene Descartes' phrase—I think, therefore,
I am.

**CONCRETE OPERATIONS STAGE OF MENTAL
DEVELOPMENT:** One of Piaget's categories of mental
development (7 to 12 years)

CONDITIONING: repeated insistence of performing some act/actions
to achieve a certain way of behaving.

CORBELLING*: This was a new stone-age* method of roofing where stone slabs overlap more than 50% of the slabs beneath them as they are placed on top of each other till they come together on all sides and are then connected with a capstone.

CORMOLOGICALLY AWARE: to be aware of oneself in relation to the cosmos; knowledge of the universe and awareness of our role or situation therein.

CREATIVE THINKING: Original thinking, or, a priori thinking

DAY-DREAMING: Unconscious, or subconscious thinking while awake and involved in some waking activity.

DEDUCTIVE REASONING: reasoning from the general to the particular.

DIDACTIC METHOD OF TEACHING: . . . . lessons are presented or dictated: hand outs and presentations are given by a teacher. The Teacher is the central person in this method.

DOPAMINE: a neurotransmitter that helps to control the brain's reward and pleasure centres.

EMPIRICAL VERTIFICATION: empiricism maintains that experience is the only source of knowledge and verificationism is a consequence of that tenet—empiricists claim that ideas that are not connected to experience and testable are meaningless.

ENNEAGRAMS: a system denoting personality types—nine types—*1 Reformer, 2 Helper, 3 Achiever, 4 Individualist, 5 Investigator, 6 Loyalist, 7 Enthusiast, 8 Challenger, 9 Peacemaker.*

THE EPISTEMIC FALLACY: is where being is understood as perceived being—statements about being are statements about what we know about being.

EPISTEMIC RELATIVISM: ontological relativism opposes just one correct version of reality; epistemic relativism objects to just one correct epistemic standard—contrary to absolutism.

EXISTENTIALISM: This is a philosophy claiming that human beings have an existence only, they do not have an essence—we are constantly in the process of making our essence—this is progressed with each moment of our existence, till death, at which time existence is terminated and essence is formed.

EXTRASENSORY PERCEPTION: perceiving through mental telepathy.

FALSIFICATION THEORY: the theory that unless you can prove something to be false it cannot be declared untrue, observation and experience are not sufficient to assert that something is false.

FORMAL OPERATIONS STAGE OF MENTAL DEVELOPMENT: One of Piaget's stages of mental development (12-15 years)

FRONTAL LOBES: one of four pairs of lobes in the cerebral cortex—a left and right—responsible for our personality—they regulate motor function, problem solving, spontaneity, memory, language, judgement, control of impulsive behaviour, initiation, social and sexual behaviour. The left lobe associated with language, the right lobe with non-verbal abilities, such as creativity and music appreciation—not exclusively, both lobes are involved in all aspects of thinking—logical reasoning and creativity.

GALAPAGOS ARCHIPELAGO: an archipelago of volcanic islands in the Pacific Ocean, around the equator some just north and some south of the equator—where Charles Darwin did research and observation for his theory of evolution.

GENETIC SCIENCE: science of genes, heredity and variations in living organisms.

HIPPOCAMPUS: in the limbic system situated in the temporal lobes—a pair—they play a major role in short and long term memory and in spatial navigation.

HISTORICITY: a philosophy that maintains nothing has meaning outside of its historical context. We are in the flow of history.

INDUCTIVE REASONING: reasoning from a specific case or cases to deriving a general rule.

INTELLIGENCE QUOTIENT (I.Q.) tests are conducted to measure a person's level of intelligence. A score of 100 is considered average 95% of population are believed to fall within a score of between 70 and 130.

INTUITIVE / PERCEPTUAL STAGE OF MENTAL DEVELOPMENT: One of Piaget's stages of mental development. (4-7 years)

LATERAL THINKING: term coined by Cherry Thomas and used frequently by Edward de Bono—creative thinking as opposed to a linear way of thinking.

METAPHYSICS: a branch of philosophy endeavouring to explain the meaning of being and the world.

NEOLITHIC ANCESTORS: people of the *new stone-age period* that started around 10,000 BC

NEOCORTEX: it is part of the cerebral cortex—the outer layer. In humans it plays a part in spatial reasoning, conscious thinking, language, sensory perception and the formation of motor instructions.

OCCIPITAL LOBES: one of the four pairs of lobes in the cerebral cortex, located at the back of the brain. It is responsible for visual perception, principally.

OEDIPUS COMPLEX: Freudian theory maintaining that boys have a sexual attraction to their mother and a desire to kill their father. It occurs in the phallic stage (3-6 years)

PARANORMAL: refers to phenomena outside the scope of scientific explanation or measurement—experiences or occurrences outside the normal range of explanation.

PARIETAL LOBES: one of the four pairs of lobes in the cerebral cortex, located at the top of the brain between the frontal and occipital lobes. It is involved primarily in spatial sense awareness. It arranges visually perceived objects.

PERCEPTUAL/SYMBOLIC STAGE OF MENTAL DEVELOPMENT: One of Piaget's stages of mental development—occurs (2-4 years)

PHENOMENOLOGY: a branch of philosophy, concerned with the study of phenomena—things as they appear in our experience. Classical phenomenologists practiced analysis of experience—lived experience, ignoring everything else. We cannot perceive essences only phenomena; that is, appearances and experiences.

POSITIVISM: sense experience and the information we gain from logic and mathematics is the source of all knowledge. It maintains that we cannot obtain knowledge through introspection or intuition.

PRAGMATISM: contrary to Positivism: We can have knowledge of values as well as of facts. Ethics, for pragmatists, is humanist; it maintains that morality outside the human context has no relevance for us.

PREFRONTAL CORTEX: the anterior part of the frontal lobes, the area of executive function. It is involved in planning and the execution of plans, decision making and personality expression. It is the area involved in thinking critically, analytically and creatively. It produces rational, as opposed to impulsive or emotional responses.

PRIMARY EMOTIONS: as produced by those advocating the theory of emotional intelligence (Daniel Goleman etc.) *joy, concern, fear, surprise, sadness, disgust, anger and anticipation.*

PROGRESSIVE EDUCATION: 'learn by doing' 'learn by discovery'. *1. Identify a problem: 2. State the problem: 3. Propose solutions: 4. Determine if the solutions would work based on past experience: 5. Set about establishing the most acceptable solution.*

REDUCTIO AD ABSURDUM: proving a proposition to be true by showing that it is impossible for it to be false—proof by contradiction (Latin: reduction to the absurd)

REPTILIAN BRAIN: located in the brain stem—the original brain in evolutionary brain development. It regulates basic needs for survival; food intake, oxygen requirements, heart rate, blood pressure, reproduction and reactions to impending danger.

SECONDARY EMOTIONS: as proposed by theorists of emotional intelligence, *optimism, love, aggression, contempt, remorse, awe, disappointment.*

SENSORY INTEGRATION DYSFUNCTION (SID) also known as 'Regulatory sensory processing disorder'. It's a neurological disorder where the processing of data from the different senses, *touch, vision, olfaction, auditory* and *taste,* is impeded or distorted.

SENSORIMOTOR STAGE OF MENTAL DEVELOPMENT—The first stage of intellectual development in Piaget's stages of mental growth—from birth to 2 years

SITUATION ETHICS: maintains that morality depends on the circumstances of the time. An action is not fundamentally good or bad, it is to be judged according to the time, place and circumstance of the act.

SUM RES COGITANS: I am a thinking being

TEMPORAL LOBES: one of the four pairs of lobes in the cerebral cortex, located on top of the brain stem. The limbic system including the olfactory system, the amygdala and the hippocampus are located in the temporal lobes. They organise sensory input, auditory perception, language, speech and memory.

TRANSACTIONAL ANALYSIS: (T.A)—it integrates elements of psychoanalytic, humanist and cognitive approaches. **T.D.** is a theory of personality and systematic psychotherapy for personal development and change. A person has 3 ego states, **parent, adult, child**—these ego-states interact in daily living. Berne's ego-states have a resemblance to Freud's **id, ego** and **superego** states of mind.

UBERMENSCH: Friedrich W. Nietzsche's term meaning 'superman'. The Ubermensch was meant to contrast with the Christian notion of the person seeking superior status in the next world. According to Nietzsche, humans are superior being, there is no God.

VERIFICATION THEORY: a theory proposed by the *Logical Positivists* of the Vienne Circle—the meaning of a proposition is determined by empirical verification—if something cannot be empirically verified it is meaningless.

VERNAL EQUINOX: an equinox occurs twice a year—vernal (spring) and autumnal (autumn) when day and night are of equal length; 12 hours daylight and 12 hours darkness.

WERNICKE'S AREA: language comprehension area, situated in the temporal lobe, generally in the left temporal lobe, Discovered in 1874 by a German neurologist Carl Wernicke.

WINTER SOLSTICE: mid winter—shortest day and longest night. Winter solstice lasts only a moment in time—the day is midwinter's day.

BIBLIOGRAPHY

Anderson, J. Secrets of the MIND: CD ROM, Focus Multimedia Ltd. U.K.

Aquinas, T. *SUMMA THEOLOGICA* English translation by McGraw-hill Publ. McGraw-hill 1964

Archer, S.M. & Collier, A. *TRANSCENDENCE* – Critical realism and God Papora, D.V. First publ. by Routledge, London, 2004

Aristotle *THE NICOMACHEAN ETHICS,* translation of **Ethica Nicomachea**. publ. 1925 – reprint 1969. London, Oxford Press.

Armstrong, D.M - **BERKELEY'S THEORY OF VISION,** published by Melbourne University Press 1960

Armstrong, T. *MULTIPLE INTELLIGENCES* 2nd edition ASCD – publ. ASCD, U.S.A. 2000

Berne, E **GAMES PEOPLE PLAY**: the psychology of human relationships. First published by Grove press N.Y. 1964 - Penguin, London 1968

Berkeley, G **PHILOSOPHICAL WRITINGS** selected and edited by Jessop, T.E London 1952 – Greenwood press N.Y. 1969

Carter, R. - *MAPPING THE MIND* Publ. in G.B. by Weidenfield S. Nicolson 1998 Paperback ed. publ. by Phoenix 2000 Fourth impression used here publ. 2004

Changeux, J.P. Secrets of the MIND: CD ROM, Focus Multimedia ltd. U.K

Chomsky, N. *LANGUAGE AND MIND* Harcourt Brace Jovanovich 1968 N.Y., Chicago, San Francisco, Atlanta, reprinted 1972

Copleston, F. - *CONTEMPORARY PHILOSOPHY* First publ. 1956 – Newman Press – New and Revised edition 1972

Dalai Lama **THE DALAI LAMA'S BOOK OF WISDOM** Published by Thorson1999

Darwin, C. *THE ORIGIN OF SPECIES* Introd. By L. Harrison Matthews, London, Dent 1972

de Bono, E. *TEACH YOUR CHILD HOW TO THINK* Published Viking 1992 - Penguin Books publ. 1993

de Bono, E. **WHY SO STUPID?** – Blackhall Publishing Ltd. Dublin 2006

Descartes, R. *DISCOURSE ON METHOD AND THE MEDITATIONS* Trans. By F.E. Sutcliffe, Penguin Books 1968

Dewey, J. *THE CHILD AND THE CURRICULUM and THE SCHOOL AND SOCIETY* - The University of Chicago Press, Chicago and London 1902 Combined edition 1956, 12th impression 1974

Dilthey, W. *THE CRITIQUE OF HISTORICAL REASON* Ed. Michael Ermarth – The Univ. of Chicago Press Published in Chicago and London 1978

Freud, S. *THE INTERPRETATIONS OF DREAMS* Trans. by James Strachey, published by Avon Books, 1980

Goleman, D. - *EMOTIONAL INTELLIGENCE* First published 1996 – paperback edition 1996 Bloomsbury Publishing, 38 Soho Square, London WIV 5 DF.

Goleman, D **SOCIAL INTELLIGENCE** First published in United Kingdom by Hutchinson 2006 Published by Arrow in 2007

Gardner, H. *MULTIPLE INTELLIGENCES* Publisher - Basic Books 1993

Greenfield, S. **THE PRIVATE LIFE OF THE BRAIN** First publ. USA and Canada by John Wiley & Sons, Inc. 2000 Publ. Penguin books 2001 reissued 2002

Hegel, W.F. *THE PHILOSOPHY OF HISTORY* Translated by J. Sibree, Dover publ. 1956

Hegel, W.F. **THE PHENOMENOLOGY OF MIND 1807**, Translated from German by J.B.Baillie, Harper & Row edition 1967

Hager, P.J. *The Critical Thinking Debate:* Editorial Introduction to **PHILOSOPHY, EDUCATION AND THEORY,** Vol. 23, No.1, 1991

Heidegger, M. *BEING AND TIME* a translation of *SEIN AND ZEIT* Translated from the German original of 1927 by J. Macquarrie & E. Robinson, publ. New York Harper & Row 1962

Hintikka, J. *Cogito, ergo sum: influence and performance* in *DESCARTES* A collection of critical essays ed. by Willis Doney Published by MacMillan & Co. 1967

Holloway, J. *LANGUAGE AND INTELLIGENCE* Publ. MacMillan, London 1951

Hood, B. **SUPERSENSE** - From Superstition to Religion - The Brain Science of Belief - First published in US by Harper One 2009 Published in UK by Constable, 2009

Hume, D. *A TREATISE OF HUMAN NATURE* 1740 – Edited by David F. Norton and Mary J. Norton, Oxford University Press Published 2000

James, W. **THE PRINCIPLES OF PSYCHOLOGY** Vol.1
Publisher: Dover Publications 1950

Lipman, M. **CRITICAL THINKING***: What can it be?* Institute for
Critical Thinking – Resource Publ. U.S.A. – Series 1, Vol. 1, 1983

Lipman, M. **MISCONCEPTIONS IN TEACHING FOR CRITICAL
THINKING** Institute for Critical Thinking – Resource
Publication, Series 2, No.3, 1989

McPeck, J. *TEACHING CRITICAL THINKING: - dialogue &
dialectic*. Published by Routledge N.Y. & London 1990.

Malcolm, N. *Descartes' proof that his essence is thinking* in
DESCARTES: a collection of critical essays. Edited by Willis
Doney. Published by MacMillan & Co. 1967

Millar, G. *PSYCHOLOGY AND COMMUNICATION
Communication, language and meaning* Edited by G. Millar.
Published by Basic books Inc. 1973.

Montessori, M. *DR. MONTESSORI'S OWN HANDBOOK* Schocken
books Inc., first pub. 1914, reprinted 1965

Nietzsche, F. *THE WILL TO POWER* – a new trans. by Walter
Kaufmann and R.J. Hollingdale – edited with commentary by W.
Kaufmann Published by Weidenfeld Nicolson, London 1967

Piaget, J. *THE GENETIC APPROACH TO THE PSYCHOLOGY
OF THOUGHT: The psychology of language, thought and
Instruction*. Edited by John P. deCecco. Holt, Reinhart and
Winston Inc. 1967

Piaget, J. *THE ORIGIN OF INTELLIGENCE IN THE CHILD*
Trans. from the French by Margaret Cook. First publ. in English
by Routledge, Keegan Paul 1953 London and Henley, 4th
impression 1979

Plato. - ***PROTOGORAS AND MENO*** Translated by W.K.C. Guthrie. Penguin books 1974.

Plutchick, R. **Secrets of the MIND**: CD ROM, Focus Multimedia ltd. U.K

Popper, K. ***CONJECTURES AND REFUTATIONS*** The growth of scientific knowledge – Published by Clarendon Press Oxford 1972

Rafferty, M. ***PROGRESSIVE EDUCATION: The Lively Corpse*** A paper by Dr. Rafferty to the 5th Anniversary Conference of the Reading Reform Foundation N.Y. – 4th August 1966 – (Speaking about John Dewey.)

Russell B, ***THE ANALYSIS OF MIND,*** London, G. Allen & Unwin Ltd. First publ. 1921

Ryle, G. ***CATEGORIES*** (1938) reprinted in ***LOGIC AND LANGUAGE*** Essays by G. Ryle. 2nd series, ed. A. Flew, publ. Blackwell, Oxford.

Ryle, G. ***THE CONCEPT OF MIND*** Hutchinson, London 1949, reprinted 1962

Ryle, G. - ***Descartes' Myth*** in ***DESCARTES a collection of critical essays*** Ed. by Doney, W. – First publ. by MacMillan & Co. Ltd., London 1970

Sartre J.P. ***BEING AND NOTHINGNESS*** **Publisher; Methuen, London 1969**

Schacter, D. **Secrets of the MIND: CD ROM, Focus Multimedia ltd. U.K**

Schrag, F. ***THINKING IN SCHOOL AND SOCIETY.*** Routledge, N.Y. and London 1988.

Siegel, H. ***EDUCATING REASON Rationality, Critical Thinking and Education.*** Routledge, N.Y. & London 1990.

Smith, A. *THE BRAINS BEHIND IT* Publ. by Network Educational Press Ltd., P.O. Box 635 Stafford ST 16 1BF 2002. Revised edition 2004

Snook, I.A. *CONCEPTS OF INDOCTRINATION* Philosophical Essays, edited by I. Snook. Routledge & Kegan Paul, London and Boston 1972.

Spinoza, B. **THE CHIEF WORKS OS BENEDICT DE SPINOZA** Published 1891 by G. Bell in London.

St. Augustine *CONFESSIONS,* with a translation by R.S. Pine-Coffin. Published by Penguin Books 1961 – reprinted 1970

Taylor, A.E. *PLATO, the man and his works* Univ. paperworks, Published in 1926 – reprinted 1971

Vigotsky, L.S. *Thought and Speech* in *PSYCHOLINGUISTICS: a book of readings.* Edited by Sol Saporta. Holt, Rinehart & Winston, N.Y., Chicago, San Francisco, Toronto, London 1961.

Willis, D. *DESCARTES* – a collection of critical essays. MacMillan & Co. Ltd. 1967

Wittgenstein, L. *TRACTATUS LOGICO-PHILOSOPHICUS* First German edition 1921 English translation by D.R. Pears and B.F. McGuinness Routledge and Kegan Paul, N.Y. The Humanities Press 1971.

Wittgenstein, L. *PHILOSOPHICAL INVESTIGATIONS* Translation by G.E.M. Anscombe. 2nd Ed. publ. Blackwell 1967

INDEX

Authors and names of people are in bold-face type

A Posteriori Thinking xxi, 64, 120

A Priori Thinking xxi, 64

Abortion 7

Activity methods of teaching 104, 109, 110

Africa 8, 77

Amygdala 11, 83, 84, 85, 86

Analytical Thinking 63, 104

Anatomy 17

Anaximander 5

Anderson, John 84, 102, 123

Antarctica 8

Anthropology 100

Aperture vii, 100, 101

Aquinas, Thomas 14, 22, 123

Archaeology 100

Archer, Margaret 79, 123

Archetypes 51, 59

Architecture 30, 33, 36, 74, 101, 119

Aristotle 61, 62, 115, 121, 123

Armstrong, Thomas 102, 123

Artists 54, 115

Atheists 74

Attention Deficit Disorder (ADD) 88

Attention Deficit Hyperactive Disorder (ADHD) 88

Aura 45

Australia 41, 77

Autumnal equinox viii, 101

Ayers, Dr. Jean 87

Berkeley, George 27, 28, 38, 123

Berne, Eric 59, 123

Biological processes 92

Biology 24

Birth Control 7

Boyne Valley 100

Brain cells 9

Brain Stem 8, 12, 82

Broca, Pierce Paul – (Broca's area of the brain) 16, 66

Buddhism 85

Burial Cells vii

C N Tower 76

Carnegie – Mellon University 84

Carter, Rita 21, 22, 73, 79, 121, 123,

Cartesian 32

Cerebellum 12

Cerebrum 10

Changeux, Jean Pierre 91, 102, 124

Child-centred education 104, 107

Chimpanzee 96

China 41, 77

Chomsky, Noam 29, 39, 124

Christianity 44, 51, 85

Cloning 7, 8, 114

Co. Meath vii, 100

Cochlear 11

Cogito Ergo Sum xi, xx, 23, 32, 38, 97, 125

Cognitive Psychology 84

Coliseum 36

Collier, Andrew 60, 79, 123

Concrete operations stage of mental development (7-12 years) 92, 93

Conditioning xi, xix, 44, 46, 48, 59, 61, 68, 89

Congo 6

Contemplatives 32, 53

Corbelling vii

Cornwell, John 120

Cortex 8, 13, 81, 82, 83, 84, 96, 113

Cosmologically aware viii

Creative Thinking xxi, 57, 64, 65, 66, 67, 82, 89, 115

Critical analysis 73, 104, 108, 110

Critical Thinking xv, 62, 63, 78, 125, 126, 127

Cyclical Order vii

Dalai Lama 120, 124

Darwin, Charles 2, 3, 7, 21, 106, 124

Day dreaming 66, 77, 89

De Bono, Edward 1, 21, 62, 63, 64, 78, 124

De Spinoza, Baruch 5, 26, 27, 31, 38, 128

Deduction 18, 27, 62

Deductive reasoning 55, 62, 72, 93

Definition of Intelligence xv, xvii, 6, 25, 81, 90, 94, 11194, 81

De-ja-vou 76

Democritus 19

Descartes, Rene xx, 14, 15, 22, 23, 24, 26, 27, 28, 32, 37, 38, 54, 56, 57, 60, 97, 98, 113, 124, 125, 126, 127, 128.

Developmental Psychology 92

Dewey, John 70, 78, 104, 107, 120, 124

Dialectic Tension 119

Didactic Method of teaching 104

Dilthey, Wilhelm 43, 124

Direct association 51

DNA 6, 7,

Doney, Willis 38, 60, 125, , 126, 127, 128

Dopamine 106

Dowth 100

Dublin xv, 21, 100, 124

Ego states 46, 47, 48

Electra complex 51

Elethia 58

Elethic truth 58

Emotional Empathy 85

Emotional Intelligence xi, xv, 81, 83, 83, 91, 102, 124

Empirical Verification xix, 25, 56, 81

Empiricism 28,

Enneagrams 45

Environmental Studies 89

Epistemic Fallacy 54

Epistemic Relativism 58

Epistemological Objectivity 54

Epistemology 58

Eros 97

Ethics 43, 58, 62, 121, 123

Euthanasia 7

Existentialism 28, 29, 98, 99

Experimental Psychology 16

Extrasensory perception 53

Extrasensory transmission faculty 53

Extrovert 52

Falsification Theory 56

Foetus 30, 31, 46

Food supplements 88

Formal operations stage of mental development (12 – 15 years) 93

Free association 51

Freud, Sigmund 50, 51, 52, 59, 112, 120, 124

Froebel, Friedrich 104, 107

Frontal Lobes 10, 11, 12, 13, 14, 15, 33, 66, 115

Galapagos Archipelago 2, 3

Gardner, Howard xx, 89, 90, 91, 92, 116, 125

Genetic Science 25

Geneticist 114

Geography

Ghost 2, 20, 36, 37, 55, 76

Gliese 581c / Gliese 581d, 4, 21

God xx, 2, 5, 20, 27, 28, 43, 44, 46, 73, 74, 98, 123

Goleman, Daniel 83, 92, 102, 124, 125

Greenfield, Susan 48, 59, 60, 106, 120, 125

Guang Yue 18

Hager, P.J. 125

Harvard University 9

Headphones 10

Health Care 89

Hegel, W.F. 43, 125

Heidegger, Martin 29, 39, 125

Heraclitus 19, 96, 99

Hinduism 85

Hintikka, Jaakko 38, 125

Hippocampus 86

Historicity xi, 41, 43, 44

Hitler, Adolf 7, 21, 22

Holloway, John 125

Hominid 15

Hood, Bruce 16, 22, 38, 56, 60, 118, 121, 125

Hume, David 27, 38, 1257

Husserl, Edmund 28, 38

Hypnosis 51, 53

Idealism 28

Indo – European 43, 44

Indoctrination xix, 44, 59, 61, 68, 70, 72, 73, 89, 128, xi

Induction 62

Inductive reasoning 62, 64, 93

Infinity 37, 95, xix,

Inner chamber vii, 100

Instinct 53, 54, 65, 84, xviii, xxi,

Institute Pasteur in France 91

Intelligence Quotient (IQ) xx, 91, 103, 111, 115, 116, xi,

Introvert 52

Intuitive/perceptual stage of mental development (4 – 7 years) 92

Involuntary Thinking 64

Ireland vii, viii

James, William 58, 60, 118, 121, 126

Judaism 85, 44

Jung, Carl 51, 52, 59

Karl, Marx 19, 20

Kilpatrick, William H. 104, 107

Knowth 100

Laboratory of molecular neurology 91

Lateral Thinking 62

Libra 4

Limbic Brain 85

Limbic System 11, 82

Linguistics 24, 29, 89

Lipman, Matthew 62, 63, 78, 126

Locke, John 27

Loco Parentis 47

Logic 5, 9, 12, 20, 23, 25, 33, 42, 55, 60, 61, 62, 69, 73, 84, 109, 114, 119, 127, xix

Logical reasoning 23, 33, 84, 119

Los Angeles 77

Louvre 76

Malcolm, Norman 126

Mammalian Brain 8

Mannerisms 88

Material World 98, viii

Materialism 19, 20, 32, 54

Mathematics 11, 89, 100

McKenna, W.R. 38

McPeck, John 63, 78, 126

Megolithic burial tomb vii

Metaphysics xvii, xviii, xx, xxi, 13

Millar, G. 126

Mohanty J.N. 38

Monotheism 44

Montessori, Marie 104, 107, 126

Multiple Intelligence, xv, 81, 89, 90, 102, 116, 123, 125, xi, xx

Music 30, 31, 32, 33, 36, 70, 74, 88, 89, 90, 91, 106, 119, xviii

Muslimism 44, 85

Neo-cortex 8, 83, 84, 85, 86, 96

Neolithic ancestors viii

Neurobiologist 91

Neurolinguistics 24

Neurological disorder 88

Neuron Cells 87

Neuroscience 16, 83, 113

New York 76,78, 125

New grange vii, 100, 101, viii

Nietzsche, Fredrich 7, 21,126

Non-verbal tasks 112

Nothingness xx, 19, 38, 95, 98, 99, 102, 127

Nurtured 88

Nutrients 88

Occipital Lobes 10, 11

Oedipus complex 51

Organ of Corti 11

Origin of Species 2, 21, 124

Oxford Dictionary 111, 120

Oxygen 1, 88

Paranormal 13

Parietal Lobes 10, 11, 12

Paris 17, 76, 77

Parmenides 5, 19

Parpora, Douglas V. 60, 79

Perceptual symbolic stage of mental development (2 – 4 years) 92

Persinger, Michael 73

Personality 21, 41, 44, 45, 46, 48, 49, 50, 52, 53, 59, 88, 89, xi, 1,

Phenomena 28, 54, 55, 57, 104, 119

Phenomenological ontology 99, 102

Phenomenology 28, 38, 125

Philosophical Investigations xxi, 128

Philosophy 5, 6, 14, 19, 20, 24, 25, 26, 28, 32, 33, 43, 44, 49, 56, 58, 61, 94, 98, 99, 100, 104, 108, 110, 118, 124, 125, xv, xxi,

Philosophy of Education 104

Physiology 17

Piaget, Jean 92, 93, 102, 126

Pineal Gland 98

Pittsburgh 84

Plato 5, 61, 96, 97, 98, 127, 128

Polytheism 44

Popper, Karl 56, 60, 127

Positivism 56, 73, 78

Potency 37, 52, 74,

Practical Philosophy 33, 49

Pragmatism 58, 104

Predators 118

Pre-frontal cortex 13, 53, 63, 64, 66, 87, 88, 106

Premise 28, 62, 69, 76, 84

Prenatal 30, 31

Primary Emotions (8) *joy, concern, fear, surprise, sadness, disgust, anger, anticipation* 84

Primates 83, 96

Prime Matter 5

Progressive Education 70, 78, 104, 127

Project work 108

Psychoanalysis 50

Psycholinguistics 22, 24, 25, 128

Psychological Assessments xx, 75, 112, 113, 115, 116

Psychologist 77, 84, 90, 91, 92, 93, 94, 108, 110, 111, 113

Psychology 16, 17, 24, 47, 59, 81, 84, 91, 111, 112, 117, 121, 123, 126,

Psychopaths 85

Psychotherapy 52

Rafferty, M. 78, 127

Rational analysis 118

Rationalism 19, 54, 20

Realism 28, 123

Reductio ad absurdum 61

Reptiles 8, 5

Reptilian Brain 8, 82

Responsive Thinking 57, 64, 65, 66, 110, 115, 120

River Boyne vii

Robert Plutchick 84, 102, 127

Rome 36, 76, 77

Rousseau, Jean Jacques 107

Russell, Bertrand 28, 38, 127

Ryle, Gilbert xx, xxi, 2, 21, 39, 54, 55, 60, 127

Saint Augustine xx, 98, 113,128

Sartre, Jean Paul 28, 37, 38, 98, 99, 102, 127

Schacter, Daniel 91, 102, 127

Schrag, Francis 127

Science 9, 11, 13, 17, 18, 24, 25, 26, 32, 37, 54, 55, 56, 72, 81, 84, 87, 89, 114, 117, 125, xi, xviii,

Secondary Emotions (8) optimism, love, aggression, contempt, remorse, awe, disappointment, 84

Secrets of the Mind CD Rom, Focus 102, 123, 124, 127

Semitic 43, 44

Sensorimotor stage of mental development (birth – 2 years) 92

Sensory Integration Dysfunction SID 87, 88

Sensory System 87

Servan–Schreiber, David 91, 102

Siegel, Harvey 78, 127

Situation Ethics 43, 58

Sixth sense 53

Skill 3, 63, 68, 72, 87, 90, 91, 106, 107, 109, 112, 116, vii, xx,

Smith, Alistair 18, 21,22, 128

Snook, I. 128

Sociopaths 85

Socrates 61, 97

Space 7, 14, 24, 27, 31, 58, 89, 95, 98, 94

Spinal Cord 12, 82

Spiritual World viii, 56, 98, 113

Spiritualism 20

Substance 5, 14, 15, 19, 24, 26, 27, 35, 52, 74, 75, 93, 96, 97, 109, 116, 117,

Sum res cogitans xx, 23, 32, 97, 120

Supernatural 25, 118

Supreme Intelligence xviii, 3, 119

Sydney 76

Sykes, J.B. 120

Tabula Rasa 27, 30

Taylor, A.E. 128

Teachers xix, 10, 16, 71, 103, 104, 105, 107,108,

Telepathy 52, 76

Temporal Lobes 11, 12, 15

Thalamus 11, 83, 84, 85, 86

The Big Bang 3, 4, 5

The Concept of Mind xx, 2, 21, 39, 60, 127

The Great Wall of China 77

The Republic 97

Theory of Evolution 2, 3, 8

Therapeutic Music (music therapy) 88

Thinking Critically 104

Tractatus Logico – Philosophicus xxi, 22, 39, 128

Transactional analysis 46, 47

Transcendence 46, 60, 73, 79, 123

Transcendental meditation 53

Ubermensch 7, 9

Verification Theory 56, 73, 78

Vernal equinox 100

Vigotsky, L. 15, 22, 128 (Vigotsky)

Visionaries 54

Wernicke, Carl - (Wernicke's area of brain) 16, 66

Wisdom xxi, xi, xix, 27, 49, 62, 103, 111, 114, 115, 119, 120, 124

Wittgenstein, Ludwig xxi, 15, 22, 29, 33, 34, 39, 55, 73, 93, 128

Zeno 61

CPSIA information can be obtained at www.ICGtesting.com
Printed in the USA
LVOW10*2227200415

435340LV00010B/273/P